Time or Tide

Time or Tide

Ali Benson Moulton

MOUNTAIN
TREEHOUSE
PRESS

Copyright © 2023 Ali Benson Moulton

All rights reserved. No part of this book may be reproduced in any form or by any means without permission in writing from the publisher, Mountain Treehouse Press, except for short excerpts used in reviews.

This is a work of fiction, based on true events and people.

ISBN: 979-8-9879479-0-6

DEDICATION

For my sisters

Nae man can tether time or tide...

　　　　-Robbie Burns

This book is based on the true story of two sisters living in Dundee, Scotland during 1842-1843. Many of the events happened as described, taken from histories and newspapers of the time. I filled in the gaps to satisfy my curiosity about why they made the choices they did. I hope you enjoy their remarkable story.

PROLOGUE

County Down, Ireland
1834

The golden leaves of the apple tree obscured Deborah's view of the road from where she perched, but she knew it was George Wright even before the long shadow anchored itself to his dust-colored boots. His deep voice carried down the road. If she hadn't been trying to hide, she might have smiled at his song. As it was, she drew in a breath and pressed her filmy violet dress along the length of the gnarled tree trunk, hoping the branches hid her from view. Rebecca's suitor was the last person she wanted to see just now.

George's body eventually caught up to his baritone and Deborah studied her twenty-nine-year-old neighbor for a moment as he approached. Dark auburn hair with a slight wave. Clean-shaven jaw. Tall frame. All wrapped up in the seen-better-days clothes of a man who earned his bread by his hands. His deep brown eyes were his only redeeming feature. They always seemed to hold a secret that you just knew would make you smile if he'd only tell you what it was.

He'll do.

Since George would probably be her brother-in-law before these leaves finished falling, she was glad he had those eyes. That was something. And he could sing. That was something, too. His jaunty song seemed to fill the orchard with a little more sunlight.

"She is handsome, she is pretty
She is the belle of Belfast City
She is a-courting one, two, three
Pray, won't you tell me..."

A branch snapped and Deborah winced. She turned her face, hoping that her brown hair pulled back into a low knot would blend in with the bark. George paused under the tree. Deborah willed him to keep walking, but he cocked his brow and squinted up into the sun. He shook his head in amusement.

"Funny apples in the orchard this year. They look a little on the scrawny side and not as sweet as usual."

"Mean. Mean. Mean. I'm as sweet as can be and you know it." Deborah found her footing and inched her way toward the ground.

"You are nowhere near the neighborhood of sweet and

you know it, lass. You're more like a green apple. A very early green apple." He held out his hand as she slid down the trunk.

Ignoring his help, she landed on the soft earth and glared at him. "Thanks for the compliment. I *like* green apples." She threw him a cheeky smile. "And so do lots of men. In fact, there's a certain one who walks along here on his way back from the fields this time of day, but you've ruined my secret lookout spot."

"You don't meet a beau up in a tree, lass. I know you've a wild heart, but even you know that," George said.

She narrowed her eyes at him, even as she took his offered arm and started down the path towards home. "You do if you danced with Danny McClelland for the first time last night and decided that you'd see him next in the orchard, awash with the glow of twilight on fall leaves. But it won't work if you are going to come clomping down the path again."

George scowled. "Then I'm glad I came when I did. Danny has half as much sense as his one-eyed mule and twice as much opinion of himself. No proper eighteen-year-old should be thinking about saying 'good day' to him, let alone meeting him in a deserted orchard. Use your noggin' Deb. You're a goose, but you know better."

Deborah punched his arm lightly and her green eyes flashed. "No need to worry about me. I don't even know why Rebecca likes you at all. You are so mean."

He leaned forward, suddenly looking more nineteen than twenty-nine. "Does she, truly? Like me, I mean. What does she say?"

Deborah rolled her eyes and let out a stream of air from her pursed lips. "If you don't know my sister is madly in love with you, then you don't deserve her. She's probably sitting by the window right now, exhaling long plaintive sighs and wondering when you are going to come see her next."

His smile returned in earnest. "Well, then, if you think she does truly love me, I'll tell you a secret." Deborah smiled and raised an eyebrow. His eyes twinkled with a real secret this time and she nodded, holding her breath. George grinned. "I'm on my way to propose to your sister."

Deborah grew thoughtful. It wasn't a surprise. A widower with two children at home wouldn't court anyone for a long time. Sarah and William needed a mother. And at twenty-eight, Rebecca was considered by most to be on the shelf, but the perfect companion for a widower. Her soft blonde curls, brown eyes, and lithe frame earned her the reputation of a neighborhood beauty, but her shyness kept her close to home. The one romance of her earlier years ended when a ship never again saw land.

No, no surprise. It would be a good arrangement for both of them.

"What is it? Will she not want me?" George stopped abruptly, panic wiping all mirth from his face.

She patted his arm. "Oh, she'll want you." She paused and

turned to him. "But can I ask you a question that I shouldn't ask you?"

A smile broke through his worry. "I'd expect nothing less from you, Deborah. Ask me anything."

Her brow furrowed and she turned to face him on the path, her fingers twisting together. She took a deep breath. "Do you truly love her? And if you do love her, do you love her because you're lonely and need someone to take care of your children, or do you truly, truly love her?"

It all came out in a jumble and Deborah bit her bottom lip as she ended, not daring to look him in the eye as the blush crept up her neck. She knew it was an inappropriate question. But she had to know. She couldn't bear to give up Rebecca otherwise.

George reached out a finger and tapped Deborah's chin up, bringing her glance to his. There was a little sadness behind his smile, but he tucked her hand back on his arm and they started towards the house again.

"Hear me out all the way? No interrupting?" he asked.

Deborah nodded.

He didn't speak for a moment, their footsteps the only sound in the fading day. "I was just a couple of years older than you when I married Ellen. I loved her practically my whole life and our marriage was the joy of my life. She was so calm and sweet-tempered, with long black hair and the bluest eyes in Ireland. When she died, I thought my soul was lost. Gone. It was that way for months. I dragged sandpaper over wood and swept up endless piles of sawdust. I sang the same song to my children night after night. I walked through the door of the church and back out again every Sunday."

A shadow crossed his face, then cleared. "It wasn't until a year had gone by that I woke up one morning and felt like the earth was a living place again. The sun was shining through the glass into my room, and I could have sworn it was the first time it had come out since Ellen left me. I remember just lying there, the light on my face, and the thought came unbidden that maybe there was still some life ahead. A few weeks after that, I noticed your sister at church. I'd heard that when your mother died, Rebecca took on that role at fourteen and raised all of you. I knew that she had a gentle disposition and would make a good mother." Deborah clucked her tongue, but George went on.

"I appreciate the goodness of everyone who helps me care for my little ones, but William and Sarah need a mother. I know that. So, when I felt like my heart could handle it, I began seeking out your sister. In complete honesty, I admit that I was looking for a kind mother for my children and hoping perhaps to find pleasant company."

He paused and took a deep breath. "What I *didn't* expect was to find room in my heart to fall madly in love with anyone again." He rubbed his hand over his jaw. "I didn't expect I could stay awake half the night like a boy just out of short pants thinking about her, that I would rush through my work to come over and watch her pour a silly cup of tea and marvel at the quiet, witty things she always says that no one seems to notice. I certainly didn't think that I'd be standing in my bedroom like a loon for two hours last night, looking in the mirror and practicing a cock-eyed speech meant to convince Rebecca that I will truly go crazy if she won't be my wife. I dinna ever think it possible, but I am very much in love with your sister and I plan on making her life wonderful."

Deborah closed her eyes for a moment and sighed contentedly. She squeezed his arm and rested her head against it for a moment.

"Oh, good."

The autumn leaves crunched under their feet as they walked the rest of the way in silence.

CHAPTER 1

County Down, Ireland
1842, 8 years later

Deborah placed a steaming circle of soda bread on the table and lifted the lid off a cast-iron pot filled with cabbage, onions, and potatoes. She couldn't help wishing there were a few plump pork sausages nestled among the vegetables. It seemed like every year the rough-hewn table was set a little lighter, but she'd not complain tonight. The room was filled to overflowing, even if the table was not. George and Rebecca brought their brood to join Deborah and her father for Sunday dinner. The meal was always a bustle with Sarah, William, Susannah, and Jamie, but she wouldn't have it any other way.

Deborah smiled at her sister, the roundness of her belly not quite hidden under the higher waist of her blue dress. She watched Rebecca tuck a stray curl that escaped her prim

Sunday bun and smile at the little boy on her lap as he tugged at her lace collar.

"Here, Rebecca," Deborah said, setting down the lid and plucking two-year-old Jamie from her sister's lap. "You eat first, and I'll help Jamie. You need to keep up your strength to grow my next adorable niece or nephew."

Across the table, her da took in a sharp breath and looked at her, hard. He set down his knife with a clatter.

"Deborah, while we are all eager for Rebecca to be healthy, a lass with manners never speaks of the delicate condition of a woman. Especially not at dinner. Especially not in mixed company. And especially not on the Sabbath."

"Though I don't see what Sunday has to do with pregnancy, I will forbear speaking of Rebecca's obvious unnamed condition, Da. But since there is nothing going on in my life except needlework, charity work, and housework, I am absolutely delighted to look forward to said unnamed event in July." She smacked a loud kiss on Jamie's fat cheek as she settled him on the skirt of her gray dress. He giggled and swatted her away. "These little angels are the brightest part of my spinsterhood."

George laughed, even as Deborah's father shook his head, apparently still reeling from the word "pregnancy" being used at dinner. On Sunday. In mixed company.

George's eyes twinkled. "You are hardly a spinster, Deb. What are you now, just thirty-two or so come next May? Truly, you don't look a day over thirty."

Deborah's head snapped to her brother-in-law, eyes fired.

Twelve-year-old Sarah, always the peacemaker, looked up from her plate. "Da! Be nice!"

Rebecca put her spoon down and looked across the table at George. "Stop it, George. She's just twenty-six and you know it." She turned to Deborah, a little smile playing on her lips. "And if you are a spinster at twenty-six, what was I at twenty-eight?"

Deborah smiled at her sister. "A spinster? No offense, but around here all the men are courting the eighteen-year-olds. They flirt and giggle like they don't have an opinion on anything deeper than the color of their hair ribbons. Besides, anyone who married me would wake up very disappointed to learn he just married a girl with half a brain."

George let out a chuckle. "Half a brain, huh, Deb? Isn't that rather generous?"

Deborah glared at him. "You know what I mean. Besides, I'd rather love these little darlings and give them back at the end of the day. And I'm assisting Mrs. McMillan more and more with her midwife practice, so I get to experience all the wonder and none of the pain of motherhood."

Her father grunted, but she ignored him. Deborah reached out to stroke three-year-old Susannah's cheek. "You don't care if I am an old maiden aunty, do you, Susy-love?" The chubby blonde pixie shook her head.

Deborah nudged her nephew seated on her right, his auburn head bent intently over his plate. "You won't mind me hanging around when I'm old either, will you, William?"

He smiled a lopsided grin that made him look older than his eleven years. "I'd love you even when you was covered in wrinkles. And warts."

Deborah faked indignation and twisted his ear. "Warts, huh? I should get some just to see how much you still love me."

Rebecca and George looked at each other across the table, and George raised his eyebrows. Rebecca gave a short shake of her head and he answered with a small nod. She took a deep breath and put both hands on the table.

Deborah leaned down to William's ear and whispered loudly, "It seems your beautiful sweet momma and mean old da are telling secrets across the table, lad." Deborah kissed the top of Jamie's black curls and looked expectantly at Rebecca. "Out with it, dear. You've always been the worst at keeping secrets."

Rebecca shook her head and breathed in slowly. She laughed nervously. "Well, I'm afraid I've been too good at keeping this one. George said I had to tell you, and I've been waiting for the right time for a month now."

Jamie's food forgotten, Deborah held the spoon in mid-air and looked back and forth between George and Rebecca.

"What secret, Rebecca?" her father asked, leaning forward, his beard precariously close to his potatoes.

Rebecca wrung her hands on the table, looking between her father and sister. She stared down at her plate. "George and I have decided that we are going to…," she paused. "That it is best for our family if we move."

Deborah let out a small sigh of relief and put down the hovering spoon. She knew the little two-room cottage just down the road wouldn't hold another baby. She may not see them as much, but she took pride in the fact she could walk the distance of the entire town without trouble.

"We're leaving Ireland and moving to Scotland. Dundee. In two weeks." Rebecca bit her lip, silence descending around the table.

The room was still. Deborah kept Rebecca's gaze, even as George broke the silence as he turned towards his father-in-law. They spoke of the opportunities a cousin had found on Scotland's east coast. Booming shipyards and textile mills. Exploding population. The prices he could charge for furniture. Renting his own shop.

Rebecca stood and walked over to her sister, planting a kiss on the top of her head. "Dear one. I'm so sorry. There was no good way to tell you."

Deborah stood and handed Jamie to his mother. She turned to glare at George, poking her finger at his chest. "That's because it is madness and you know it."

George returned her look, steady. He spoke to his daughter without breaking his gaze. "Sarah let's have you and William take the babies outside to play for a spell."

Deborah bit her cheek while the wide-eyed children walked past her, then whipped back to George. "How do you think Rebecca is going to take care of all those children and handle a newborn without me? And what if labor is hard again? She pushed for three hours with Jamie!" A grunt sounded behind her and she turned briefly. "Sorry, Da." She turned back to George. "I'm a midwife, or almost one. Have you thought of that, George? Have you thought that she needs her sister by her side?"

She turned to Rebecca. "And you! I heard you promise Momma that you'd take care of me. I was just four, but I heard it. Rebecca, I can't do without you. Without all of you. I'll die." She sat down hard on the chair and buried her wet face in her hands. Rebecca sat down next to her and stroked her back.

Her father stood and hit his hand against the table. "Enough theatrics, Deborah. You'll not guilt Rebecca into staying with you like you're a wee child who needs to be cared for. You're a grown woman who should find your own husband and care for your own babes. George has a large family to provide for. He'll do it in the way he sees best and..."

Deborah's head popped up, deaf to her father's speech. She rose from her chair and knelt in front of Rebecca. She took her hand. "I'll come with you, Rebecca. I'll share a bed with Sarah and do all the cooking and cleaning. Then I'll be there when you deliver and as long as you need me afterward. You know that you'll need me. Please, please say I can come."

Rebecca brought Deborah's hand to her lips and smiled, even as tears came from her own eyes. "Sweet Deb. I'll miss you more than anything, but I won't have my sister as a housemaid. We'll manage and we'll come back when things are better in Ireland. There's no opportunity here right now for a tradesman. And Da is right. You have your own life to live. You already spend too much of yourself on us."

Deborah snatched back her hand and stood to face her brother-in-law, wiping a hand across her eyes. "I know I drive you crazy, George, but you don't want some backward midwife or unfamiliar doctor attending Rebecca. You can't let just anyone bring your sweet babes into the world. She needs me. You know she does." Deborah paused, looking deep into his eyes. There were secrets there again, unreadable. He was considering it.

Just deciding the whole of my future.

She didn't break his gaze and lowered her voice to a whisper. "Please, George. Please don't leave me behind."

The silence stretched on for a few moments. George ran his hand over the stubble on his chin and turned to his father-in-law. "Could you manage without this caterwauling female for a few months, Da? I do know that Rebecca is comforted with her sister nearby during her confinement."

Her father gave Deborah a hard look. "Ever since she was wee, I've never liked giving the lass her way after an outburst like that." He paused and shook his finger at her. "You're too old to carry on like a banshee, Deborah!" He turned back to George, rubbing his hand across his forehead. "But it does make some sense to have her on hand to help. I can manage without her if Rebecca agrees."

Deborah and Rebecca turned to each other at the same time. They dissolved into a hug, both crying.

"Well, there's your answer, Da." George looked at the older man, a twinkle back in his eye even as he let out a long sigh. "We'll take Deborah along to Dundee." He shook his head at the sisters. "And heaven help us."

CHAPTER 2

Dundee, Scotland
1842, 2 months later

Two months later, Rebecca and Deborah walked arm in arm along Fish Street in Dundee. The day's catch filled the air, mingling with ocean, animals, and jute. Deborah took a deep breath, drinking in all the new smells that announced they were in a city.

George leased a shop at 20 Bucklemaker Wynd with a small apartment over his carpentry shop. Though the Wynd was off the main road, the clatter of horse hooves and nighttime sounds of the pub one street over kept them awake for several nights when they first arrived. Now, the sounds of the city blended into a constant din.

Rebecca startled as a horse let out a loud whinny behind them on the street. She put her hand to her chest and shook her head. "I don't know if I'll ever get used to living in the city, Deb," she said, adjusting her shopping basket. "There is always so much noise!"

"I just love it," Deborah retorted. "I never knew a place could feel so alive." She inhaled again, soaking up the pleasant cacophony of humanity and industry. "Every time I pass a new person on the street, I realize how bored I was with all the same people. Here, you could sit on any corner and count fifty new faces in a day."

A strikingly handsome man with pitch-black hair walked past them. His knitted blue gansey stretched snug around taut muscles. A deeply tanned face and strong build suggested he was headed for the wharf. He caught her appreciative eye and winked at Deborah as they passed.

Rebecca gasped quietly. "Did you see that, Deborah? Bold as brass!"

Deborah tossed her head back and laughed. "But isn't it wonderful, Rebecca? Wouldn't Da just die to see how different things are here?"

"Different isn't always better. But I will say that I love the variety of things we can purchase on our street. Kitchen staples two doors down! And ready-made cloth. I could spend George's money as quickly as he makes a sale."

"Which is often," Deborah added.

"Isn't he doing well? I've never seen him happier, set up in his own shop with as much work as he can handle. He told me he turned down a large order until next month. Would you imagine three months ago he'd be turning down jobs?"

Deborah nodded. "He's done well, Rebecca. You know he'd work the skin off his hands to provide a nice life for you. I've never seen a man so smitten, even after eight years of marriage. I have to give him that, though he's a big meanie to me."

Rebecca smiled indulgently. "He's a good man, Deborah. And he's not mean to you—you just goad him all the time. George is like a little boy sometimes. I can tell by the way his eyes sparkle he enjoys getting you fussy."

"Aye, some days I can hardly tell him from William."

Rebecca laughed. "Except for the ruggedly handsome face and big, strong arms and…"

"Enough! I think I'll be sick on the street. You can keep your romantic musings to yourself." Deborah looked up at the street signs. "Just two more blocks. Are you feeling well?"

Rebecca subconsciously put a hand on her belly. "I'm fine, Deborah. Though I have to say I'm uncomfortable out in public in such a state. I feel everyone is staring."

"At your beautiful bump of a baby? Let them stare. And thank you for the reminder; I wanted to see if the bookstore can order an obstetrics book Caroline Bethune told me about. It's written by a man, but has some worthwhile ideas about labor and delivery."

"I'm grateful you've found a midwife looking for an assistant, Deborah. Caroline seems to be a good sort," Rebecca said.

The sisters crossed the street, dodging a cart. "She's been a godsend. She's more interested in medical advances than silly folk cures."

A large sign proclaiming their arrival at Chalmers Bookstore greeted them on the next block. A small bell tinkled as they pushed open the heavy wooden door and a slim man with graying hair popped out from behind a bookshelf to greet them.

"Welcome, ladies! If you dinna find what you're needing, just come and ask. I have it, or I can get whatever you're wanting."

Deborah nodded her gratitude, taking in the rows of volumes. She walked towards a center display and pressed a large volume to her chest. Rebecca glanced at the spine of the mottled brown book as Deborah placed it in her basket. "More Robbie Burns?"

"We're in Scotland, Rebecca! Who else should I read? Besides, I can't help it. I'm in love with him. He's passionate and earthy and expressive. He loves the beauty of nature and is obsessed with the women in his life. He's simply divine." Deborah sighed.

Rebecca laughed gently. "I think you just described your dream man." She winked at her sister. "Maybe that's why you haven't yet married. Robbie Burns is no longer available."

The sisters took their time choosing a fairytale book for the younger children and drawing paper for Sarah and

William. Deborah noticed that Mr. Chalmer ended up in whatever aisle they chose, pulling out and re-shelving random books. His friendly smile had hardened, and his eyes tracked all their movements.

Deborah and Rebecca headed to the front counter. Deborah looked around, surprised that the proprietor hadn't followed them after his awkward vigilance while they shopped. After waiting for several moments, she rang the small bell on the desk. Mr. Chalmer came toward the desk, but disappeared behind the counter and into a back room. After a few moments, he made his way to the register, wrapped their purchases sloppily in brown paper, and snatched Deborah's coins from the counter.

Deborah and Rebecca exchanged a glance, and Deborah cleared her throat. "I'm delighted to see your fine collection of poetry, Mr. Chalmers. I've been looking for this volume of Burns."

He didn't look up and set Deborah's change on the counter, avoiding her outstretched hand. "Aye. We Scots are a very literate people." He plunked the packages into the basket on the counter and walked into the backroom.

Deborah opened her mouth, eager to retort the idiocy of implying that Irish customers buying *books* were *illiterate*, but Rebecca grabbed her arm and the basket in one motion. She propelled them through the door, setting off the merry bell in their wake. Somehow, the noise of the street was more welcoming than the silence they'd left behind.

They were both quiet for some time as they headed toward home. Rebecca spoke first. "Well, Mr. Chalmer was certainly more attentive when he welcomed us in than when he hurried us out."

"I'm sure it had nothing to do with our Irish accents." Deborah spoke through tight lips.

"George's cousin warned us, but I'm still surprised by how many smiles fade as soon as they hear us speak. I didn't realize how much some people truly dislike the Irish." Rebecca said.

Deborah took a deep breath. "I think 'hate' is a better word. Part of me wanted to snatch back our money and storm out of the shop, Rebecca. If I hadn't really wanted Burns, I would've left him in a huff. I'm still shaking!"

"Aye. Scotland and Ireland are just a stone's throw apart from each other, but it doesn't seem like they're interested in being particularly good neighbors."

Deborah sighed. "Well, I hear there's another bookseller in Peter's Court. We'll see if Mr. MacIntosh has better manners." She linked her arm with Rebecca's and they walked home in silence.

"Time for poetry lessons!" Deborah shouted as she opened the door. There was a mixture of groans and cheers as

Deborah set down her basket and planted herself in the rocking chair, grabbing Jamie onto her lap. She kissed the toddler soundly on the cheek and snuggled Susannah to her side. William and Sarah came from the table and sat on the floor as Rebecca moved to the stove and pulled a rough-woven bag of potatoes from the pantry box.

"More school?" William dipped his head glumly. "We just got back!"

Rebecca gave the eleven-year-old a pointed look. "Do your studies well with Aunt Deborah and I'll boil a clootie dumpling tonight, love."

"With sultanas?" three-year-old Susannah asked.

"Lots," Rebecca responded. The children brightened considerably. Susannah plunked down on Sarah's lap, leaning back against the twelve-year-old.

Deborah opened the book and consulted the table of contents, flipping the pages to the poem she was after. "Listen to this sweet little story. It's about a farmer plowing his field and turning up the nest of a little mousie:

Wee, sleekit, cow'rin, tim'rous beastie,
O, what a panic's in thy breastie!
Thou need not start away so hasty,
Wi' bickering brattle!
I would be loath to run and chase thee,
Wi' murd'ring paddle!
I'm truly sorry man's dominion,
Has broken nature's social union,

An' justifies that ill opinion,
Which makes thee startle
At me, thy poor, earth-born companion,
An' fellow-mortal!"

After several pages, Deborah clapped the book closed with a sigh and looked at the children. "Don't his words just sing a song?"

William shrugged and stood.

She patted his arm. "Well, anyway, let's help get the table all dressed for dinner. I heard your stomach growling."

Deborah moved towards the table as a small knock sounded at the door. She opened to a stout, white-haired woman holding a fragrant parcel wrapped in a white cloth.

"Mary! I'm so glad you found us!" Deborah moved aside for the lively package of black silk and sunshine to pass.

Mary placed one hand on her heart as if to pat down the palpitations. "Aye, I've found you. You and the only flight of stairs these old legs have climbed in a blue moon. I think you'll be needing to visit me on the ground from here on out."

Deborah smiled and motioned Mary into the room. "Rebecca, this is my new friend, Mrs. Mary Carse. She lives three doors down on Bucklemaker Wynd."

Susannah walked up to the stranger. "What's in the cloth?"

Rebecca wiped her hands on her apron and hung it over a chair. "Susannah, remember your manners, dear." She turned to Mary and held out her hand. "I'm delighted to meet you, Mrs. Carse. Deborah told me so much about you. It sounds like you've had some lively discussions."

Mary chuckled and squeezed Rebecca's hand, then bent down to hand the sweet-smelling parcel to Susannah. "This, my dear, is a treat called Scotch petticoat-tails." She placed it in Susannah's hands and pulled back the cloth. "Do you see the design of the biscuit? It looks a bit like the large hoop petticoats that fancy ladies used to wear." She covered the treat. "Can you put it carefully on the table so you can spoil your supper well and proper?"

Susannah nodded and ran precariously with the parcel towards the table. Mary rose and turned to Rebecca. "It *is* best eaten warm, luv."

"I'm sure it won't have time to cool in this house," Rebecca said, glancing toward the children already gathered around the table. "Sarah, we'd best be saving your da a piece." She turned to Mary. "Did you meet George on your way in?"

"Did I! Lass, he was just doing some sanding on a bench, but I swear he was trying to stop this old heart of mine with those big strong muscles rippling as he worked." Mary fanned her neck as Rebecca's face flared red.

Deborah laughed and linked her arm through Rebecca's. "That's why we have to keep him locked up below." She winked at Mary. "Otherwise, Rebecca would never get a thing done."

Rebecca swatted at Deborah, her face aflame. "Oh! I think the two of you are a heap of trouble together."

Mary laughed. "The first time I met Deborah, we talked for an hour about a woman's right to property and education and what it would take for men to wake up and recognize their equals. We may have a few decades between us, but we're cut from the same cloth. Mine is just a prettier tartan pattern."

"It's true," Deborah said. "I'm so glad to have found a kindred friend in Scotland." She grinned. "Especially one who bakes."

Mary glanced at the children, picking at the treat on the table. "Speaking of, I dinna want you to miss a nibble of those biscuits. They were a special favorite of my late husband, and quite divine if I do pat myself on my own back. I'll leave you alone to sneak your sweets before dinner."

"It was so kind of you to stop by, Mary. I'm grateful to finally meet you." Rebecca squeezed her hand again. "Do you need help down the stairs?"

"Oh, I'm not that decrepit yet. But if I stumble, I'll just call out and fall into your handsome husband's arms." Mary winked as she passed through the door, the children's sugar-sweetened smiles following her.

Rebecca closed the door and turned to Deborah, shaking her head and laughing. "She's what Da would call a firecracker."

Deborah grinned. "And he wouldn't mean it as a

compliment. I think she's just delightful." She took Rebecca's hand and leaned on her shoulder. "She's the medicine my soul needed tonight. It's good to remember that some people are good and kind."

"Most," Rebecca said. "Most."

CHAPTER 3

"Have you seen this?" Deborah thundered down the back stairs and burst into the store. George looked up from his workbench, stain-covered cloth in hand.

He put the rag down. "And a fine morning to you, too. What's put you in a tizzy now, Deb?"

"Have you read the article in this morning's *Courier* about a new book by Mr. James Myles?"

"Does it look like I've been reading much this morning, lass?" George held up his stained hands somewhat impatiently over the small oak cradle that sat on his workbench.

She ignored his remark. "Mr. Myles has some devilish opinions of we Irish who've made Scotland our home. Listen to this! 'It is deeply to be lamented that the vast hordes who have migrated are composed of the most debased and ignorant of their countrymen. Their vile slang and immoral habits have seriously injured the general character of the poor population of Dundee. The low Irish are not a very improvable race. They cling to their rags, their faith, and their filth with all the besottedness of perfect ignorance and stupidity. They appear impenetrable lumps of humanity. The customs now prevalent amongst the poorer classes on Sunday are all derived from the examples of the vulgar Irish who within the last fifty years have deluged all the manufacturing towns of modern civilisation.'"

She slapped the paper down on a nearby table. "Ignorant fool! Things are bad enough for the Irish without stirring up the public with such lies. I've a mind to march into the *Courier* offices, shove this paper down the editor's throat and demand a public apology for printing such tripe."

George leaned an elbow on his workbench and sighed. "Isn't it the way of man? Trying to hide the wickedness in their own souls by pushing it onto someone else. They pile up the burden of vice on the backs of the poor and downtrodden, so they don't have to face it in themselves."

Deborah cocked her head, thinking about the idea.

George gestured towards the newspaper on the pine table. "Kindly remove your paper from that table, lass. It's not quite dry yet." He picked up his rag. "And kindly refrain from giving this Mr. Myles any more ammunition against the Irish by exhibiting your wild Irish temper. I can see the next *Courier* headline now: 'Lunatic Irishwoman demands greater kindness and compassion towards the Irish by strangling Chief Editor.'"

Deborah picked up the paper, hoping George wouldn't notice a few letters from the newsprint imprinted into the lacquer. "I will refrain from violence, but I *will* write a letter to the editor, protesting the publication of Irish slander." She slapped the paper across her hand and smiled. "And I'll hand-deliver it with a smile and a warm loaf of Irish soda bread, all dressed up in my Sunday dress with a new bonnet. I have some coins from assisting Caroline Bethune with her last two deliveries, just begging to be spent."

"Sounds like visiting the editor is a nice excuse to buy a new bonnet," George said wryly, moving the cloth back and forth over the small cradle.

"Anything for justice." She smiled as she crossed the room and ran up the stairs two at a time, George shaking his head behind her.

CHAPTER 4

Not an hour later, Deborah caught her reflection in the window as she exited Walter Foyer's Hatting Establishment on Reform Street. She turned her head to admire the new green bonnet that sat atop her head and adjusted the bow under her chin. Two rows of shirred ruffles framed her face, and a large bow that Rebecca would surely pronounce as ostentatious covered the back. She missed shopping with her sister, even with her more conservative tastes, but Rebecca had pled swollen feet and declined the trip. Deborah knew that Rebecca, seven months into her pregnancy, didn't enjoy being seen in public too often in her "delicate condition," but she'd invited her just the same.

Deborah took one more look at herself in the window, admiring how the green bonnet complemented the light brown dress she'd selected, with its long, dropped sleeves and ribbon crisscrossing down the center of her torso to end at a tucked waist.

She had no illusions about being a beauty, but she knew that her shapely figure drew attention. She often coveted Rebecca's silky blonde curls, but today her unruly brown hair had been on its best behavior, staying put in the woven mass that peaked from her bonnet. Deborah gave herself one more look and smiled, imagining the editor's face when a well-dressed Irish woman came to make a protest call. She would follow George's advice and not cause a scene, but she fully intended to turn a head or two. The injustice of the morning was long forgotten in her excitement as she started down the street towards the editor's office, relishing the afternoon sunshine. She was glad to have a few blocks of travel to collect her thoughts.

"Now, that's a bonnie smile with a story behind it."

Deborah turned sharply to the right to see the same black-eyed man she'd noticed a few days ago leaning against the rough stone of a barbershop. His clean-shaven face and black wavy hair suggested he'd just come from the establishment. "I'd love to hear the thought that inspired such private happiness."

"'Private' is the keyword, sir." Deborah lifted her chin and continued walking, resisting the urge to look back at the man, who chuckled as she clipped away. She heard his footsteps behind her, but still jumped when she heard his voice.

"Begging your pardon. I dinna mean to offend you, lass, but you had the most intriguing look on your face. I figure you're either plotting sweet revenge or dreaming of your lover." His voice gave him away as distinctly Irish, but his use of Scots suggested he wasn't a newcomer. He matched his pace with hers and came up beside her.

She stopped and turned to him. "I *don't* want a lover, I *am* plotting–just a wee bit–and *we* haven't been introduced. Good day, sir." She couldn't resist matching his grin, even though she lifted her nose in the air and picked up her pace.

The man laughed again and ran ahead into the blacksmith shop three stores ahead. As Deborah came abreast of the store, the stranger came out with a burly, ruddy figure wiping his hands on a soiled white apron. The large man smiled through his whisker-covered jowls and bowed low to the ground as Deborah passed.

"Hello, lass. Alexander Lawson here, master of iron, nails, and stove grates if you're ever in need of such. May I have the pleasure of introducing a fine, upstanding, law-abiding citizen named...Charlie Martin?" Her follower nodded. The man turned to Deborah. "And Mr. Martin, may I introduce this fine lass what goes by the name of...," he gestured expectantly at Deborah.

She threw back her head and laughed. "Deborah Hasley, sir." She dropped into a proper curtsey.

On her way up, Charlie raised an eyebrow. "Now that someone has properly introduced us, let me escort you wherever in this fine city you've a mind to go with that delightful smile on your face." He held out his arm. The blacksmith grunted in amusement as he turned back to his business.

Deborah hesitated just a moment, then placed her hand on the crook of his arm. The firmness of his arm surprised her and she decided her initial estimation was correct. Definitely a sailor. "Sir, you may escort me to my final destination, then I must beg leave."

"I'll take it, lass." He put his hand over her hand on his arm. "Where to?"

Deborah took three more steps and pointed to the *Courier* sign above her head. "Right here. It was a lovely walk, but we seem to have arrived already. I thank you for your kind escort." She sent him a cheeky smile and unhooked her hand from his arm. She waved goodbye as the bell jingled at the entrance.

Serves you right, you outright flirt. This time she did look back to see him watching her walk away with an appreciative smile. She turned away, taking the soda bread and a letter to the editor from her basket.

Deborah sweetened her smile even more as she approached the leathery, ginger-haired man with heavy lambchop sideburns behind the dark wood desk.

"Hello, Sir. I'd like to talk to the Editor if you would please direct me." She smiled demurely.

He looked down his nose at her, exposing a bald spot

shining in the middle of his mass of curly hair. "He's expectin' ya?"

"I should think so!" *Surely, anyone who had published nonsense would expect some response.*

He gestured his head to the left. "Through the first glass."

She thanked him, then walked towards the glass door, taking a deep breath filled with paper, ink, and bustling bodies. Deborah shifted her parcel and pushed the door open confidently, striding to the enormous mahogany desk and the slight, middle-aged man who sat dwarfed behind it.

"I beg your pardon?" His nasal voice was quiet, tinged with annoyance.

"Good morning Mr.," Deborah glanced at the brass plate askew on his desk, "Hutton. I've come to discuss yesterday's *Courier*."

He sighed and stood, his blond head coming as high as Deborah's nose. "And you'd be Irish, I'd wager."

"Proudly, Sir. I'd like to discuss the rubbish you've printed in the last several months that spawns misconceptions about..."

He raised a hand, swatting her comments from the air. "I've nothin' against the Irish as a whole, Miss. My grandmother was, in fact, from County Cork." His blond head tipped slightly to the side for a moment and a small smile raised one side of his mouth. "I've even hired Irish newsies. No one can call me prejudiced. But my job is to sell newspapers. To tell the news. And the news is that Scots are feelin' overrun. Nervous about the rise in the Catholic population. Overburdened with the poor comin' in. They're upset. That's the news and I'll stand by it."

"But surely you could...," she began.

"I'm not running a charity. Now, I've work to do. Awa' w' ya, lass." He sat down and dipped a quill in ink.

Deborah took a breath, heart pounding in her ears. She reached into her basket with trembling hands and pulled the round loaf of fresh soda bread out, wrapped in clean linen. She plunked it in front of him.

"Enjoy this, Mr. Sutton. May it remind you of your Irish grandmother who would be so proud of your decision to lend a hand to the downtrodden and oppressed. Good day, Sir." She turned on her heel and pushed the door open. The metal frame crashed against the stopper. She turned to make sure the glass was intact and saw Mr. Hutton break off a corner of the warm loaf. He sniffed it, plopped it in his mouth, and dipped his quill.

For the first few blocks, she was angry. But sadness prevailed for the rest of her walk home. She felt so in-between. She'd made some friends here, her Protestant religion binding her to the Scots. If she went back far enough, her County Down roots even reached across the water back to Scotland. The countries were historically intermingled, as evidenced by Mr. Sutton's family history. But now, walking down the street and looking into the faces of her neighbors, she felt a separation growing. Would they smile and nod in her direction if they knew where she was born?

CHAPTER 5

The apartment above George's carpenter shop seemed to shrink in the deluge of rain. Rebecca didn't feel well and seemed a little frayed with the noise of her two youngest. They darted through the kitchen, overturning a chair in their wake.

Rebecca set the chair upright and grabbed Susannah's arm. "Susannah, stop chasing Jamie this minute. He had the wooden horse first and you played with it all morning." Uncommon bite tinged her voice. Jamie hid the horse protectively under his shirt as he tore across the room. Rebecca sighed as Susannah followed him.

Deborah grabbed Susannah as she ran past and cuddled her on her lap. "Enough, Susannah. Let's take a break, shall we? I think the rain has stopped for a bit. Want to go down to the docks to see the ships?"

The little girl nodded. "Da big ones?" She asked, eyes wide.

"Aye. The big ships are getting ready to go out on the ocean and hunt for whales." Deborah affirmed.

"Da big ones?" Susannah asked again.

"The big ships or the big whales, dearest?" Deborah asked.

"Da big whales!" Susannah nodded.

"Aye! They hunt for whales that are so big they would fill this whole house and several more on either side!"

Susannah wrinkled her nose. "I'm glad dey live in the water, and not in a house!"

Deborah laughed. "I'm glad, too. Otherwise, we might have to sleep in the ocean!"

Susannah was silent and furrowed her brow. "Den I'm glad dey hunt the whales so I can keep my house."

Rebecca walked slowly toward the door, a hand massaging the side of her swollen belly. She took down two small sweaters from a hook. "No whales are coming to your house, luv." She turned to Deborah and mouthed a thank-you and she pulled Jamie from under the table and brought him to the door.

Deborah smiled back and wrestled one of Jamie's shoes on. "You should do this yourself, Jamie! A big boy of two like you."

"I know we need the whale oils, but it is sad to see them haul in those creatures." Rebecca mused.

"I agree. They are so magnificent. But," she continued with an innocent raise of her eyebrows. "If we didn't have whaling boats, we wouldn't have so many sailors in town. And I *really* like having all the sailors in town."

Rebecca lowered her head into an expression Deborah easily recognized.

And now, my dear sister morphs into my fussy mother.

"I'm sure there are some very nice sailors, but from what I've seen so far, they are a rough-and-tumble crowd. If there's a commotion on the street, nine times out of ten it is a group of sailors, drunk and happy or drunk and angry. They are a rowdy bunch and I'm not much impressed."

"Rebecca! How many times have we talked about the injustice of the Scottish judging the Irish as one whole group? Some Irish people are good, hard-working folks, and some are troublemakers. It isn't fair to lump us all together. And now here you are doing the same thing to sailors! I think many of them are quite charming and well-mannered. And," she lowered her voice, "they are the best-looking men in the whole city."

Rebecca lifted her chin. "I prefer carpenters," she said simply, kissing her two youngest on the head as they headed out the door with their aunt.

The trio stomped down the stairs. Despite the disagreement, Deborah felt happy as she took a chubby little hand in each of hers and stepped out into newly-washed Dundee.

She let Jamie and Susannah run ahead of her to stomp in the big puddles the storm had created on the uneven cobblestone. The sun broke through and she lifted her face toward the warmth. She stopped to breathe in the fresh air; the smog temporarily trampled down by the sweet spring rain. A snatch of the poem she just marked the previous night ran through her mind.

Amang the trees, where humming bees,
At buds and flowers were hinging, O,
Auld Caledon drew out her drone,
And to her pipe was singing, O...

"You wouldn't consider holding still for a moment or two, would you, lass? You are a bit of perfection right now in that patch of sunlight."

Deborah knew who the voice belonged to before she turned to see Charlie sitting on a bench. He still wore the low hat and tight-knit sweater of someone acquainted with the sea, but now had a sketchbook in hand.

Her eyes widened in surprise and she took a couple of steps closer. "You are an artist, then? I had you pegged for a sailor."

"Guilty on both charges. But truly, you are a picture of contentment just waiting to be drawn this morning. I'd love to capture you."

She raised an eyebrow. He grinned and winked. "On paper, of course."

Just then, Susannah and Jamie came running towards

them in a cascade of splashes and giggles. Deborah smiled at their enthusiasm, but Charlie snatched back his drawing pad as a drop or two landed nearby. He swiped his arm in their direction.

"Gee awa wi' ya! Can' ya see yer splashin' mud on the fine lass's gown and me sketchbook?" His angry voice stopped the children like a wall. Their smiles fell and Deborah opened her mouth, shocked at his anger over a few drops.

"But we hadda show you the baby worms we found." Susannah's lip trembled a little as she looked up at Deborah, tears forming in her big brown eyes. Deborah reached down and lifted her chubby hands.

"Aye! They are lovely wee baby worms, Susannah! What a good finder you are. I know you didn't mean to splash, dearest." She kissed her cheek and turned to Charlie. "May I introduce Susannah and Jamie? Children, this is Mr. Martin. He is a sailor and, apparently, an artist."

Charlie stared at the two children, faces now hidden in the folds of Deborah's skirt. He closed his sketchbook with a snap and smiled thinly. "My regrets for my outburst and my improper comment, ma'am. I didn't realize you were a mother. Good day."

How easy to just leave it there. Deborah hesitated for another moment as he turned his back to her. "They are my sister's children, Mr. Martin." Her voice was quiet, but she knew it communicated more than the volume showed. Why did she feel she was the fisherman now? Hook tentatively cast into the calm of the water, not knowing if she hoped for a bite or not. Wanting the tug, but not sure what to do with the fish.

A slow smile came back on Charlie's face as he turned back towards her, his head tilted slightly to the side, sizing her up. "Well, then."

Deborah ducked her head with the blush that crept up her neck and busied herself with extracting Susannah and Jamie from her skirt. She spoke quickly before she changed her mind. "If you'll excuse us, I promised the children a walk to Dock Street to see the ships."

"And who better to show a ship than a sailor?" He turned to Jamie. "How would you like to hear how we nab a whale, laddie?"

Jamie looked up at Deborah, who nodded encouragingly. He turned shyly to Charlie and nodded.

The quartet walked towards the water, the children careful to avoid the puddles. Part of Deborah mourned the loss of their freedom, but she was proud of their good behavior. She walked with a child in each hand, but was highly aware of Charlie at her side. She hazarded a glance in his direction, appreciating his strong profile and athletic build. She schooled her gaze, but not before Charlie noticed, and smiled a slow, delicious smile.

Keep it casual. "So, do tell us about life aboard a whaling vessel, Mr. Martin. I ken it isn't an easy one."

"It's hard, but it is the most exciting place a man can be."

They arrived at the docks, and Deborah smiled at the activity that surrounded them. Against the sea wall, three businessmen, topped with black hats and cinched by tight silk vests, inspected a shipment of wooden crates. Their bright cravats stood out in contrast to the roughly woven cloth tied around the necks of the sailors who collected the straw the men scattered in their perusal. A man who looked like someone had scraped him from the seafloor itself pushed a rickety cart toward a small dingy. He veered to avoid a stately couple out for a walk, a bright blue parasol shielding the woman from rain that might change its mind.

As they waited for a small herd of brown-spotted cattle to plod in front of them, Charlie leaned down to Jamie and pointed at a large vessel gently bobbing in the morning waves.

"Do you see the small boats on the side?" he asked, leading them closer after the cattle passed.

Jamie nodded and answered in a small voice, his eagerness overcoming his residual anxiety. "What are da small boats for?"

Charlie sat down on his heels, "Those small boats are how we catch a whale, lad. Imagine hearing the cry of 'Whale!' then heaving yourself over the side of a black and white ship into one of those six boats right there. Then you're lowered into the churning ocean and you're rowing towards a massive shape just under the surface. You ken that shape is either going to make you a very rich man, or a very dead one.

You see the spray blow up from below and you cast a harpoon into the dark flesh. The rope gives a tug and suddenly all the men in all the boats are casting harpoons. You say a prayer that the monster doesn't decide to dive and drag you away into the fog, never to see land again. As the whale fights, the harpoons dig deeper into its flesh for hours and hours. You finally get close enough to spear the beast through the lungs, and it is almost over. He thrashes his tail in the water once, twice, three times maybe, then rolls to his side."

He stood up, rowing his arms. "Then you row back to the ship and haul him up. You pull out a big knife and cut off large slices of blubber and cram them in a barrel. Next, you harvest the baleen from his jaw and stow it away. After that, all's left is to heave the bloody carcass back into the ocean with a big splash."

He hooked Deborah with his gaze. "Then you finally come back into the docks after weeks and weeks away, with a pocket full of shillings, a great need for a bath, and a notion to find the prettiest girl in town and tell your tale." Charlie put his hands into his pockets and smiled, satisfied.

Deborah looked down at Jamie to find his eyes wide and mouth half-open. She smiled up at Charlie faintly.

Well, that was a little more detailed than expected.

She opened her mouth to speak when Susannah took three deep gulps of air. She looked up at Deborah, her innocent eyes filling with tears.

"Den day cut dem all up?" She let out a sob, the tears overflowing down her chubby cheeks.

Deborah kneeled on the hard cobblestone and pulled Susannah close. "Shhh now, Susannah. Remember, they're already dead, so they don't even feel a thing."

"Dey don't know dey's cut all up?" She raised her teary eyes to Deborah.

"Nope. They don't know a thing. They are already happily swimming...," she hesitated, hopeful her impromptu doctrine was at least a ha'penny shy of blasphemy. "They're swimming in whale heaven, where there aren't any whaling vessels at all." She looked up at Charlie and cocked an eyebrow. "And no whalers." She smiled hopefully toward the child. Susannah took comfort and nestled back under Deborah's chin, the sobs subsiding.

Charlie was silent as Deborah eventually stood, brushed off her skirt, and grasped a hand in each of hers. "I, uh, dinna ken it would upset her. I didn't tell the half of it..."

Deborah smiled genuinely. "Well, we'll save the other half for another day, shall we? When there aren't tender ears around."

Charlie took a step closer until Deborah could pick up a trace of his cologne, something spicy with citrus. *Since when do sailors smell good?* She took a deeper breath and leaned towards him, which Charlie took as an invitation to take another step closer.

Her eyes widened a bit and she swallowed hard, keeping

his gaze. "Aye. I'll tell you the rest when we're alone," he muttered quietly, his gaze intensifying. Then he smiled his crooked smile and winked at her. "' Till then, can I walk you back home? We'll just talk of sunshine and butterflies, shall we?" He smiled down at Susannah, who scowled at him in return.

Deborah stifled a laugh and leaned toward Jamie and Susannah. "Would you like to run ahead a bit and look for more worms?" They didn't need a second prompting, their shoes clipping the cobblestone walk. "But no splashing!"

"Well played, lass." Charlie held out his arm and she tentatively raised her hand to take it as she led him home.

CHAPTER 6

It was Friday night and Charlie said he would stop by for her. She had seen him several times since the day at the wharf, but this was the first time he had officially come courting.

Deborah carefully examined her small store of dresses, finally settling on a deep red one with trim all up the bodice and surrounding the hemline. She'd borrowed Rebecca's nice shawl and spent extra time tressing her silky dark hair into a dignified pile, heating the iron over the stove to form little curls at her temple. She was ready. Still, Deborah jumped at the knock at the door. She strode towards it, but George passed her in a few long strides. He reached the door first and put his large hand on the latch.

"I'll say hello first, lass." He smiled at her with a look of authority.

She lowered her voice and narrowed her eyes at him. "I am twenty-six years old, George, and I don't need a keeper. You aren't my Da."

He met her gaze for gaze. As they stared each other down, Rebecca breezed past both of them. She opened the latch and greeted Charlie with a cheery smile. "Hello, I'm Rebecca, Deborah's sister. Do come in, Sir."

Charlie looked tentatively at the unexpected welcoming committee, then stepped forward. He bowed slightly to Rebecca. "Pleased to meet you, Ma'am." He stuck out his hand to George, who took it with vigor. "And you must be George." He glanced down at the rough hand that still clasped his.

Maybe a little harder than necessary, George? Deborah rolled her eyes. *Men!* She turned and smiled up at Charlie as he extracted his hand. "I'm ready. Shall we go then?"

"Oh, but we've just met Charlie," George said. "I believe I saw that the performance at the Theatre Royal starts at eight, so you'll have plenty of time. Why don't you sit a while and chat a bit?" George smiled at Charlie, but it didn't reach his eyes.

Charlie met his steady gaze. "I wish I could, but I promised friends we'd meet for a bite to eat before the play. They're probably at the pub right now. Another time, then?" He put his hand on Deborah's back and ushered her toward the door. "Good to meet you both. Have a good night." He nodded to Rebecca and they were out of the door before

Deborah could even catch her breath.

"I'm afraid I've already eaten, Charlie," she said.

He grinned. "We're not heading to the pub, Deborah. I just wanted you all to myself, love." He rubbed his hand. "And I thought he was going to rip my hand off with his friendly handshake. Right charming guy."

Deborah grinned. "George isn't so bad, but he is a strange combination of an older brother, father, and protective friend all wrapped up in one. Triple trouble." She linked her hand through his arm. "Don't worry about him. Rebecca keeps him tame. She's the dearest, isn't she?"

"Aye, she is. And almost as beautiful as you." His eyes scanned her face appreciatively. "But not quite. You look lovely tonight, lass."

Deborah blushed and looked down. *I hardly remember how to behave!*

They chatted as they leisurely walked to Castle Street. Deborah was aware of glances from women and girls of all ages that followed them as they passed. She sneaked a glance at Charlie. He had shed his sailor's hat, usually pulled down low over his head, and instead wore his head bare. The black waves hung down a little over his forehead and blew with the gentle breeze. His clothes looked new, no doubt a result of payment from his recent whaling expedition. Indeed, he was a handsome man. *And here I am, walking through town on his arm.* The thought made her almost giddy. As they reached the Theatre Royal on Castle Street, her excitement grew. The building rose before them, two stories of theater over four small shops beneath.

"I've read Othello several times, but I've never seen it. And to see Ira Aldridge as Othello! I've never seen a black man on stage."

Charlie raised an eyebrow. "I dinna ken black men played Shakespeare."

"Of course they do! They didn't accept him where he was born—in New York—or in London, for that matter. I've read some of the scathing reports from the *Times*. It's a big pile of rubbish and prejudice. Most people agree that he's one of Britain's finest actors. And he's here in Dundee, of all places!"

"Well, I dinna ken much about that, but I ken I'm lucky to have the prettiest woman in Dundee all to myself tonight." He squeezed her hand on his arm and drew her a little closer.

"They say that his da is a clergyman in New York, but that they are descended from a line of princes of the Foulah tribe from Senegal. Can you believe it? An African prince! And he's playing one of Shakespeare's most complicated characters. Imagine being so full of passion and jealousy that you would kill the very thing you love most! It's one of the hardest roles to play, and I've read that he is the very best."

Charlie raised his eyebrows and pulled away slightly. "Or imagine that you're trying to tell a lass how beautiful she is, and she's going on and on about an African prince?"

Deborah was silent for a moment, then pursed her lips. She turned to him. "I'm sorry for rambling, but it seems that the 'green-eyed monster' may be here already."

"I dinna ken what you're talking about, but that pretty little pout makes me not care too much." He leaned in closer and spoke slowly into her ear. "I don't think you know just what an attractive woman you are. You really must have been holed up above that shop these past months for no one to have noticed that yet."

Her skin tingled with the feel of his warm breath on her ear. "I've not been holed up, I've had no notice that interested me until now, and..." she paused, turning to whisper back in his ear, "The play is about to start." She pulled back with a saucy smile.

"Cheeky." He said ruefully. "Alright, lass, let's go see this passionate Othello that has you so excited tonight." They climbed the stone steps and entered a large lobby.

Deborah gasped quietly as they passed through the doors into the Theatre Royal. "There must be over a thousand people here! I don't know that I've ever been somewhere so grand in my life!"

"I thought you'd like it, love," Charlie said, leading her into the ticket booth. "We're for two in a center box, if ya please."

The man in the box looked up behind a glass window. "Do you know how much a center box is, laddie?"

"Aye, and even Irishmen like a place for their backsides to land instead of joining the masses of highland coos standing the whole time in the center of the theater," Charlie spat back.

The man narrowed his eyes and placed the tickets in front of him, holding them with two fingers. He named the price and Charlie got the coin from his pocket. Only then did the man release his hold on the tickets. Charlie plucked them from the counter with a scowl.

He was silent on his way to their seats. Deborah looked straight ahead, calming her breathing. "This is beautiful. Look at those curtains."

Charlie didn't comment, so she fussed with her small handbag for a moment. The silence stretched on. Deborah cleared her throat. "Well, he seemed to like us, didn't he?"

"I've a mind to go back and toss a brick through his glass window."

Deborah put her hand on his arm and tried to be casual. "But then, I'd miss seeing Ira Aldridge as Othello, and I'd have to walk home alone as you're carted off for a night in jail."

Charlie's narrow mouth slowly curved up in a smile. "Well, since I want more than anything to see you home tonight," he glanced at her lips, "I guess the glass is safe."

She felt her cheeks warm, but hoped the darkness hid her high color. Just then, the curtain lifted, and another world opened up.

The play was everything she had hoped for. When Othello realized the deceit that led him to kill his precious Desdemona, his anguished cry brought tears to her eyes. Charlie reached over and took her hand, bringing it back to rest on his leg. Although the theater was dark, she looked around. She knew no one could see her, but still. He rubbed her knuckle with his thumb, and she was almost distracted from Othello's final speech by the sensation.

At the end, she stood to applaud, clapping eagerly as the curtain fell. She turned to Charlie, her hands pressed to her heart. "Thank you. Thank you so much! That's the highlight of my time in Scotland. What did you think?"

"Well, there was plenty of action, but all the lovely ladies get the knife. That seems a shameful waste."

Deborah paused. "That's hardly the point, Charlie."

He took her elbow and led her from the box. They saw the actors gathered near the exit, greeting the patrons as they exited. Charlie tugged her towards the other side door.

"I'd love to meet the players, Charlie."

"You mean you'd love to meet *him*, don't you?"

"Aye, I'd like to meet Mr. Aldridge. But," she lowered her voice conspiratorially, "if he asks me to run away with him to Africa and claim his rightful throne, I promise I won't until *after* you've walked me home." She swatted his arm. "Don't be so silly and jealous!"

Charlie frowned at her. "I'm not jealous. Let's go meet them."

Deborah propelled them towards the crowd until they stopped before a tall man. As she turned, Deborah met his deep brown eyes. Ira wore stage makeup and his face was covered with a tightly curled beard. His right ear held the earring of Othello and a white cape trimmed in gold draped across his body, a sharp contrast to his ebony skin.

Deborah held out her hand and shook his. "Your performance was simply superb. I loved every moment."

Ira nodded graciously. "I thank you for coming."

She looked at Charlie, standing silent beside her. She nudged him a little with her elbow.

"Aye. Nice work. It must be nice for them to save on makeup. Imagine turning some Scottish redhead into a Moor." Charlie smiled at his joke.

"On the contrary, friend. It is easy to make a white man black, but it is a dirty job to make a black man white. When I play Macbeth, they try to powder me away."

Deborah paused, reading the meaning in his eyes for a moment. She sensed Charlie shifting at her side. She smiled quickly. "Well, I hope we get to see your Macbeth in Dundee one day. Thanks again! It was truly a memorable night."

She let Charlie take her by the elbow and lead her down the stairs. Once they were outside, she snatched her arm away and folded her arms in front of her chest as she clipped down the sidewalk.

"Now, why the sudden January frost, lass?" Charlie bumped his shoulder with hers.

"The only thing you could comment about was his skin color? He is a famous actor, Charlie, highly regarded throughout Europe. He's played in all the major theaters. Do you think he isn't tired of only being known for his skin?" She stopped walking to glare at him.

Charlie put his hands on her upper arms. "He didn't seem offended, so I don't see why you should be." He slid his hand down her arm, his eyes pleading. "Come on, Deborah, let's not ruin this perfect night."

Deborah gave him a conciliatory nod but kept both of her hands together on her bag for the short walk home. They made small talk, but the evening lost some of the magic that had crackled the air on the way to the theater.

When they reached 20 Bucklemaker Wynd, she turned to Charlie. "Charlie, it truly was one of the most exciting things I've ever seen. Thank you so much for inviting me." She reached her hands out to take his. He opened his mouth to speak, but she squeezed his hands and turned to unlatch the door, and stepped across the threshold. "Thanks again! Goodnight!"

Deborah bit her lip and leaned against the closed door. She knew he meant to kiss her, but she felt conflicted. There was no denying her attraction to him, but there was a harshness about him she couldn't easily reconcile with the tenderness.

I guess that's what happens when you live on a boat with only men most of the year. She played the thought over in her mind, making it become true. She touched her hand where his rough thumb had caressed her skin during the play. She held it to her lips for a moment, then made her way upstairs.

CHAPTER 7

Sunday was living up to its name, with warm rays streaming through the window. Rebecca sat in the rocker by the glass-paned window, soaking up the light, a volume of poetry in her hands. Sarah sewed a doll dress at the table with Susannah while Jamie napped.

Deborah sat on the floor with William, her blue dress bunched beneath her, a wooden puzzle between them. Her mind wandered back to the night before. She woke up this morning miffed with Charlie. The sunshine seemed to cast a different light on his outburst at the ticket counter and his awkward comment to Ira. She replayed the events in her mind over and over as she should have been listening to Reverend Ewing at church. She knew Charlie was disappointed that she hadn't left any room for a kiss, but his behavior had thrown cold water on any previous ardor. She smiled, remembering the look on his face as she'd slipped inside the house.

William waved her hand in front of her face. "Halloo, Aunt Deborah."

She concentrated again on the wooden pieces on her lap and the black-haired child in front of her. "Let's see, William...I think this piece goes right here!" She placed the shape in her hand into the puzzle with a satisfying click.

William did the same. "And now this one fits!"

Deborah tousled his hair, which he immediately pawed back in place. They turned their attention to the pile of pieces and surveyed the board.

"Your da didn't mean for this to be an easy one, did he?"

"I told him the last one was too quick for the big kids. He's testing me." William said with a grin. "He's going to be so surprised to see that we got it all done."

Deborah had never known a father who would take the time for such frivolities, but George was a gifted carpenter. He must have spent long hours with his coping saw to create this treasure for his children.

Rebecca drew in a short breath and turned her head sharply, "Deborah! Robbie Burns wrote some very naughty poems!"

Deborah tossed her head back and laughed. "I know! Aren't they delightful? You may want to skip a few. But there are so many others that are just perfection." She turned to the girls sewing in the corner. "Just look at Sarah and

Susannah. Didn't he just capture their contentment?

With small to sell and less to buy,
Above distress, below envy,
Oh who would leave this humble state,
For a' the pride of a' the great,
Amid their flaring, idle toys,
Amid their cumbrous noisy joys?
Can they the peace and pleasure feel
Of Bessie at her spinning wheel?"

Deborah sighed. "And make sure to read *To a Louse*. You'll never sit in the back of a woman in church again without looking for an 'augly, creepin, blastit wonner.'"

"I have no idea what you just said, Deb. Some of his phrases roll right over my head." She closed the book and set it on a small table near the chair. "I think I'm done for now, but thanks for sharing."

Rebecca stood as if her belly led the event. She placed her hands on her hips to bring the rest of herself along and groaned. "I swear my confinement is coming any day now."

William looked up at Deborah and whispered. "What's confinement?"

Deborah stole a glance at Rebecca, busy at the stove. She leaned down and said quietly, "It's the proper word for a pregnant woman delivering a baby and needing to stay at home to rest and recover."

"Recover from what?" William whispered.

She leaned in closer, sure that Rebecca wouldn't

appreciate the conversation. "How do you think it feels to push a baby out of yourself, sir?" Deborah asked.

William grimaced and went back to the puzzle. "Where does this piece go?"

"You try to do the rest. That way, you can claim all the credit and brag to your da about what a smart boy you are." Deborah smiled at him and gathered herself up off the floor. She walked to the stove and placed a hand on Rebecca's abdomen. Her gaze shot up. "Rebecca! The baby has dropped! A full hand's worth. Do you feel any differently?"

She lowered her voice to a whisper. "Differently as in, 'Do I feel like there is a brick wedged in my lower regions?' Aye. I feel differently. I've visited the privy five times already today."

Deborah looked at Sarah who had picked up the book of Burn's poetry and started reading at the table. "Sarah, love, please check the bread that it doesn't burn. I need to check your momma's baby in the other room." She raised her eyebrows at the book in her hand. "And don't read the naughty poems."

Rebecca slapped her arm. "You could just say that we need to talk, Deb!"

Deborah laughed out loud. "Are you still trying to hide the fact that you are pregnant, dearest? Sorry, but I think that secret is out. Come waddle into your bedroom and let me see how this little one is doing."

Rebecca smiled faintly. "Women just don't talk about

such things in public, Deborah."

Deborah's smile vanished. "That's why women face childbirth wholly unprepared, scared, and dangerously uninformed, Rebecca. It is a perfectly natural and wonderful process. It shouldn't be hidden and scandalized." Deborah took a deep breath. "Lectures later. Exam now." She stepped aside for Rebecca to enter the room.

Deborah pulled out her midwife's bag. She checked Rebecca's vital signs and recorded them in her small notebook. She pressed down on her stomach, smiling when she felt a kick. "Are you saying hello to your auntie, luv?" She smiled when she felt the baby's head low on Rebecca's abdomen. "Good. She's still head down."

"She?" Rebecca asked, amused.

"Just a feeling. But you know that I'm always right." She winked and continued to feel the baby's kicks. "Nice and strong. That's great." She glanced at Rebecca after counting the kicks for a few moments.

"I think I'm enjoying the Scottish name for a midwife better than the Irish. I like the sound of being a 'howdie' instead of a 'handy-woman.' It has a nicer ring to it."

Deborah helped Rebecca sit up and looked at her deeply. "Baby's doing great, but your color isn't very good, Rebecca. How about you stay in bed for a bit today? It's cool and quiet in here. Sarah and I will finish dinner before George comes upstairs."

Rebecca smiled. "It does sound easier to stay put than to

move. Thanks, Deborah. Thanks for everything." She reached up and took her hand. "I can't believe we even considered coming to Scotland without you. My dear sister and my very own howdie. I don't know how I'll ever thank you."

"By staying healthy and letting me help bring another darling Wright baby into this world. That's how." Deborah ran a hand over her sister's face and headed for the door, closing it gently behind her. She shushed James and Susannah who were scuffling over the same wooden horse. "Momma is resting now. Let's make her a picture, shall we?"

The children were happily settled at the table with their paints when Deborah heard George singing a hymn from down below, coming home from an evening church meeting. His deep voice echoed up the stairwell with a hymn Deborah recognized from *Harmonia Sacra*.

"The winter's night and summer's day
Glide imperceptibly away,
Too short to sing thy praise;
Too few we find the happy hours,
In haste to join those heavenly powers
In everlasting lays."

The last line resonated as he entered. His glance around the room registered Rebecca's absence immediately. "Is Rebecca well?" His voice came out quick and a little frantic.

Smitten old fussbudget. "Aye, George. Your darling is

resting. The baby has dropped so she's a little uncomfortable. Delivery is probably not more than a week or two away." She caught the worry in his eye. She rose and walked across the room to where he still stood near the doorway. She placed her hand on his arm and spoke quietly. "George. She is doing well. The baby is healthy. She is healthy. You need to trust that things will be well. She'll get the best care possible."

"There are no guarantees." He said quietly, his gaze settling across the room.

"No. There aren't." She squeezed his arm. "You know that better than anyone. But there is no reason to borrow worry. You know I'll take good care of her."

"Aye, Deb. I do." He patted her hand on his arm. "I'm glad you're here for her, lass."

"Supper's ready!" Sarah proudly took the lid off the cast iron pot she'd placed on a metal trivet on the table.

George washed at the small basin and then took his seat at the table. "Perfect timing, love. I could eat a wee horse right now."

Sarah grinned. "Not a large one?"

"No, lass! I'm not that hungry. A wee one will do just fine." He lifted the lid and took a long sniff. "But if a wee horse isn't available at present, this lovely Dublin Coddle will do just right." He took a long whiff of the pork, onions, apples, and potatoes. "It smells divine, luv." He smiled up at his daughter. She went back to the stove for the bread and placed it on a small carved board in the middle of the table.

Sarah beamed at her father's praise and scooped the tin plates full of the simmered mixture. The spices filled the air and brought something akin to contentment to Deborah. It smelled like home, Ireland, and having enough to eat. She had a stray thought of worry skit across her mind about Rebecca's delivery. Her other labors had been excruciating, and Deborah knew that Rebecca wasn't strong. This baby even felt larger than the others. But she did believe in what she told George. She smiled and held out her plate for the stew, determined not to borrow trouble. She, of all people, had to be calm and confident. She'd seen laboring women fall apart when the pains began. She'd also seen hysterical women soothed by calmly whispered instructions from a confident midwife. It was her job to be strong, even with her doubts.

A knock at the door interrupted her reverie. She hurried to open it before the noise woke Rebecca. She flung the door open, expecting to send a neighbor child scampering back home with a reminder that the Wright family didn't play on the Sabbath. Instead, black eyes met hers and lit up at her surprise. Charlie smiled a slow smile and handed her a bundle of wildflowers tied with a length of twine. His voice was low and melodic. "I saw these in the fields outside of town and thought they were almost as lovely as you." His eyes roamed across her face, then glanced behind her.

I can just imagine the face George is making.

Charlie raised an eyebrow and tipped his hat towards the group at the table, then turned his attention to Deborah. He leaned against the doorframe. "I see you're sitting down to eat, so I'll be on my way. I'm thinking it's a right fine night for a walk tonight." He looked as if he might say more, but just nodded his head again and slipped away down the stairwell.

Deborah stared after him then turned, flowers in hand, towards the spectators at the table.

Sarah put her hands to her mouth and let out a squeal. "Oh! How positively romantic! Is that who you went to the play with, Aunt Deborah?"

Deborah nodded as she headed to the cupboard for water. She felt a deep blush under George's stare, hoping he didn't know how her heart was beating. She set the flowers in the center of the table and calmly said, "Please pass the bread."

George shook his head and let out a puff of air from his tight lips.

Deborah snapped towards him. "George, if you say one thing, I'm leaving the table. How many times have you pushed me to get out of the house, make some friends, and 'be young, lass'? Dozens! And now that I've made a… friend…you try to break his hand and glare at him across the room. They are just flowers." Her voice softened, and she fingered a colorful bloom. "I've never gotten flowers."

George's expression softened a little as well, but he shook

his head. "And you deserve to get them. I'd just prefer that a pleasant farmer or shopkeeper was handing them over. Maybe Nathan down the street or another merchant from church. Charlie has a look about him I just don't like. I've known too many like him."

Deborah rolled her eyes. "You decided all that in the two minutes you've seen him? Come on, George. Leave it be. Trust me."

George glanced at the children, listening in rapt attention as their heads bobbed back and forth between their father and aunt. He cleared his throat. "Sarah, scoop your da some more Dublin Coddle, love. Even though you forgot to add the horse, it is mighty fine."

The meal progressed without further discussion, but Deborah felt a blush light up her cheeks every time she looked at the flowers sitting in the vase. She'd flirted plenty when she was younger, but at twenty-six, she hardly knew how to respond to such attention. She kept quiet the rest of the meal and only half-listened to George bantering with the children and coaxing Jamie to eat a few more bites.

CHAPTER 8

After she washed the dishes, Deborah peeked in to see Rebecca still dozing. She closed the door quietly. She headed to the small bedroom she shared with the girls and stared at the woman in the mirror. She tucked a rebellious strand of hair back into the high braid and patted her dark hair into place.

Deborah bit her lip and turned her head from side to side. She pulled the strand of hair back out to frame her face, loosened the braid, and tugged a few more curls down her back. *Better.* Her hands splayed across her middle, noting the extra flesh that had accumulated while she hadn't been watching. While she had been busy.

She sighed and turned from the mirror. She left the bedroom with a quiet click of the door and lifted her chin, finding a comfortable smile for George. He sat in the rocker by the window, a Bible in his hands. "Well, I'm off to get a bit of fresh air. It's such a warm night. I think I'll go look in on Mary Carse then maybe take a walk."

He looked up at her, tension in his eyes. "Aye, Deb. It's a nice Sunday evening. I bet Perth Road is especially nice."

She narrowed her eyes. "It is such a lovely Sunday tradition for courting couples to walk along the very public Perth Road. Maybe I'll be like Mr. May and go watch them for a bit. Have you seen him? He's a sweet little man, very poor and as simple as can be. I asked Mary Carse about him, and she told me he's on Perth Road every Sunday. He sits for hours, watching the courting couples stroll by. It's like he's at the finest theater or concert hall. It's just charming that he thinks young people courting each other is a wonderful and proper thing, don't you think, George?"

George shook his head, sorting out which words had a chance. "Deborah, I've nothing against courting. It's just what Rebecca and I want for you." He paused and looked her solidly in the eye. "But I don't like Charlie. At all."

He stood up and turned towards the window. "I know you'll still walk out that door right now because you're flaming Irish and young and tired of being cooped up all day. I know I share some of the blame for that, letting you take so much responsibility here." He turned to her again. "But please, lass. You aren't eighteen, and this isn't your da's apple orchard."

"Noted, George. But I don't think you'd even like me

walking about with the Pope." She smiled and headed towards the door. "Please look in on Rebecca in an hour or so and make sure she doesn't need anything." She closed the door behind her and leaned against it for a moment. She walked down the stairs and out the door, breathing in and out deliberately. *He's probably not even there.*

But there he was, leaning against the brick just outside George's shop entrance. A huge smile lit up his face as he walked towards her.

"Good evening, Miss Wright. The Scots have a tradition of walking their lovely companions up and down Perth Road on Sunday." He held out the crook of his arm. "Would you like to add a few Irish to the mix?"

She took his arm with a warm smile. "Aye, I would, Charlie. I happened upon the tradition quite by accident a few weeks ago. I felt a little awkward and went over to the next street to continue my walk."

"You? Walking alone on Perth Road? What a waste." Charlie clucked his tongue and shook his head and propelled them across the quiet street. After a moment of silence, he ducked his head towards her, his dark hair falling across his forehead. "So, someone hurried off a little abruptly last night." Deborah started to speak, but he continued. "I thought it through, and I ask for your pardon. I dinna ken that any man likes to hear the girl on his arm praising another man to heaven, but I acted poorly and I'm sorry."

Deborah smiled up at him, mollified. "Well, you didn't

know that it would upset me. I guess we're just getting to know each other, aren't we?"

Charlie matched her smile, "Aye, lass, we're just getting started." Something in his eyes made that maddening blush creep up her neck again. He laughed softly. "You have no idea how charming your blush is, Deborah. You'll turn me into a rogue, just trying to bring that pretty color to your face."

Deborah knew her blush deepened. She shook her head. "Oh! Talk about something else. How did you spend your day?"

"Well, I darkened the doorway of a church for Mass to please my mother, then went for a pint to please my father. I took a walk and gathered flowers to present to the prettiest girl I ken, then spent an hour lingering outside her door. Hoping she would ken that I was waiting for her. Hoping that her crotchety brother-in-law wouldn't lock her inside. Hoping that she would ken that I was sorry. Hoping she'd take my arm on Sunday afternoon. Hoping I could see her blush again." He laughed as her cheeks flamed.

"Well, here I am."

"Aye, here you are."

They strolled up and down Perth Road until the sun dipped below the buildings and the other couples dwindled. Deborah learned more about his family, about the quiet mother and loud father he lived with when he wasn't on a whaling ship. About the two sisters who teased him as a boy, and married the same summer he went to sea at sixteen.

"I sometimes wonder if I'd be a better sort if I hadn't spent those years surrounded by men. I could've probably used a bit more time with my mother and sisters around. But I ken whales. I've never lacked for work, even in a country that would prefer the Irish were at the bottom of the sea instead of riding the waves. They ken I'll chase the monsters 'til they roll and not run back to the ship like a new sailor worried about being pulled into the deep for good with only water to mark his grave."

"I'm sure you are a wonderful whaler, but I do feel a bit sorry for the whales. They are such majestic creatures."

Charlie let out a stream of air. He gestured up to the glowing gas light they passed under. "You don't feel sorry that you have fuel for your lamps on the street or in the argand lamps in the theater. You don't feel sorry that the fabric for your fine dress was woven on machines greased with whale oil." He glanced, slow and steady up and down her figure. "And I don't feel sorry that corsets are made with flexible whalebones. I think I'm making a mighty fine contribution to society when I bring down a whale."

Deborah gasped and looked around. "Charlie! You can't just say..."

He chuckled as Deborah tried to snatch her hand from his arm, but he held tight. He brushed a gentle kiss on her knuckle. "Don't pull away, Deborah. I promise to behave. We'll even get you home before dark so that your keeper doesn't call the peelers to form a search party to come to find you." He placed her hand back on his arm and guided them toward the shop. He kept his other hand over hers as they walked, drawing an occasional circle with his thumb that sent shivers up her arm.

They reached the shop, but Charlie guided her past the entrance and into the deeper opening of the shop next door. The shadows from the fading sun gathered in the dark doorway. She let go of his arm and folded her arms across herself. *Breathe, Deborah.* She looked up at him and caught her breath. He was standing so close, she was sure he could hear her heart racing.

She willed her voice to be calm, but it came out low and trembling. "Thanks for the walk, Charlie. And for the flowers. It was a lovely night."

He reached out and brushed a finger across her cheek. "Oh, Deborah. You fold your arms so primly and say, 'thanks for the walk,' but you have no idea what your dark eyes are saying." He took another step closer. She moved back a step, but her back pressed up against the brick. Her hands came behind her, pressing against the coldness, steadying herself.

She tried to keep her voice light as she looked up at him. "Oh? And what are my eyes saying without my permission?"

His lips were on hers before she even registered the movement. They were warm and tender but became more insistent as he felt her response. He pulled her closer, pressing her to him as his hand splayed across her back. She spent one delicious moment soaking up the sensation of his mouth on hers, then pulled back, her breath short and ragged. He planted a soft kiss on her forehead and nuzzled her hairline down to her ear. He tipped his head again, but Deborah backed away. She looked up into his flaming eyes.

"Goodnight, Charlie." She slid along the brick, her hand gliding down his arm.

He turned and pressed his shoulder to the brick, tugging her gently towards him. She smiled and squeezed his hand one more time. "Goodnight," she whispered.

He pulled off his hat and ran his empty hand through his thick curls. "Goodnight, Deborah."

Deborah walked the few steps to the back door and opened it quietly. She hurried inside and refastened the latch. She faced the stairs to their apartment but pressed the back of her head against the door as a big smile spread across her features. *What a kiss! No, George, I'm definitely not eighteen anymore.*

Deborah waited a few moments for her breathing to slow down and for the heat to leave her face. She slowly ascended the stairs and entered the family's apartment. Everyone was gathered around the table for their Sunday tradition of Bible reading.

"Hello, luvs." She pulled out a chair and stroked Sarah's hair as she sat beside her. "I'm glad I'm in time for reading."

Rebecca looked back and forth between George and

Deborah. Her sister discreetly shook her head at George and his lips thinned. She turned brightly to Deborah. "It looks like the weather was nice tonight, Deb."

She smiled at the ever-diplomatic Rebecca. "It *was* a lovely night, thanks." She looked directly at George and held out her hand for the large leather Bible. "Now, where are we? I'll take a turn."

He slid it across the table to her with his finger on the verse she had interrupted. She began reading in a casual voice.

And so, the evening passed in peace. How she longed to take Rebecca into the other room, grab her hands, and squeal with her as they'd done in earlier years. But Deborah could feel the tension between Rebecca and George and knew it was about her. She wouldn't do anything to upset the balance and distress her sister. With a baby coming in just a couple of weeks, Rebecca needed to be as calm as possible right now.

So, Deborah just readied for bed and burrowed into her quilt, smiling.

CHAPTER 9

Deborah turned towards Charlie's sketchbook. He pulled it towards his chest. "No peeking, lass."

Deborah shook her head and smiled. She settled her gray silk skirt on the barrel and looked towards the Bay of Tay, stealing a sideways glance at him. He leaned over his paper, his usual cheeky smile replaced by a quiet intensity. His dark waves fell over his eyebrow as he looked down and then back up at her again. She'd miss him this week as he sailed for England tomorrow on a merchant ship. He was done with whaling for the summer, but he picked up small jobs through the fall and winter.

She liked this side of him, serious with his pencil in hand. This beautiful Tuesday afternoon together had been an unexpected treat between jobs, and they had spent the whole day together. Their Sunday walks were an unspoken date, usually the only time she saw him between his time on ships or at the wharf, and her responsibilities with the children.

"Eyes at the Bay of Tay, if you please, lass. I know it's hard to take them off me for a moment, but you'll have to try." He reached over and pulled a strand of hair loose from the low knot at her neck.

She rolled her eyes, but obeyed. "When did you start sketching?"

"I think it was somewhere during my first journey to sea. There are only so many ropes to coil and boards to polish on a ship. There is a lot of time between catches. Boredom enough to drive a young man to watch another sailor sketch and boredom enough to drive him to try. I found I had some aptitude, and it made the quiet hours pass pleasantly enough." He put down his pencil and smiled a crooked grin. "But drawing sea birds and weathered old sailors isn't nearly as fun as studying every line and curve of your face. There certainly isn't a mouth like that anywhere on a whaling ship." She blushed under his scrutiny and he chuckled.

"Now, if I was a painter, I could capture that blush. Pencil doesn't quite do you justice."

She was content to watch the water as he finished, taking in the stillness of his admiration, the quiet bustle of industry in the background. The sun warmed her face, contentment seeping through her skin. Eventually, he stood and offered her a hand. He pulled her up and brought her close to him, kissing the top of her head. "Ready for the big reveal?"

She nodded eagerly, and he turned the sketchbook around, holding it in front of his chest. She gasped slightly.

"Charlie! It's like looking in a mirror! You have such talent."

He beamed, obviously pleased with her reaction. "It's easy when the subject is so lovely, lass." He reached out a hand and traced a line from her ear, stroking the soft skin under her chin.

"You could draw anything, Charlie! Oh! Let's go back to Rebecca's! The children would just love to have their likenesses drawn. You could get one or two of them done before you have to go. I bet Sarah especially would be delighted. She has taken to spending hours in front of the mirror, trying different hairstyles. She thinks she's quite the lady now at thirteen."

Charlie's smile faded. "Though being surrounded by a pack of lively Wright children sounds like a delightful way to spend the last couple hours I have with my girl, I'll have to pass this time."

Her face fell. "Are you sure, Charlie? They would love it."

"Deborah, you are with them too much as it is. I get you for one more hour before I sail out, and you want to go home early and spend our time getting jumped on and tugged around by that bunch of children."

He looked mistreated and dejected. "Don't you want to

spend that time with me before I have to go away again? I won't see you for so long."

Deborah lifted her chin. "You are positively pouting, Charlie. We've just spent the whole afternoon together!"

He tore the drawing from his pad and thrust it toward her. She took it, her mouth open to speak, but he cut her off.

"If you'd rather go play nursemaid, that's up to you. I'm sure you'll have a delightful evening." He pushed his sketchbook and pencil into his shoulder bag and took her hand, squeezing it. "Goodnight, Deborah. I'll see you in a week."

She stood on the dock for another moment, processing their conversation as his boots clipped away. She considered calling out to him, but he slipped into Mickey Coyle's Public House without looking back.

Last week, she saw him spill out of the establishment and onto the sidewalk with a clump of sailors. Their drunk and raucous laughter filled the street, and she pulled William to the other side. Charlie hadn't seen her, but the sight disturbed her. She knew that most men frequented the pubs, but both her father and George shunned alcohol, so it had been foreign and unsettling to see Charlie staggering.

She sighed and walked the few blocks home herself. The relative quiet of the street echoed the clip of her heels on the cobblestone and the setting sun lent a peaceful, rosy glow to the top floor of the buildings. When she was with Charlie, his charm absorbed her niggling concerns. But this quiet, this aloneness, allowed uneasiness to seep through the cracks again. She longed to talk to Rebecca about Charlie more openly and wished she didn't feel compelled to smooth and polish her accounts of their time together.

Deborah turned the corner and glanced at her reflection in the glass storefront of the barbershop where she first talked to Charlie, wondering what he saw when he looked at her. She studied herself a moment longer, searching for answers to questions that ebbed in her mind. *Well, he certainly keeps things interesting.*

She shook the remaining frustration from her shoulders, straightened her posture, and lifted her chin.

As she entered the shop a few moments later, she could hear the sounds of laughter seeping through the floor. It sounded like an elephant was taking tea with the family above. A smile found its way back to her face as she climbed the stairs. She opened the door to find George on the floor, with Susannah and James on his back. He was bucking like a bull and trying to throw them to the ground. They squealed in delight as each one tumbled off their ride onto the hand-woven rug. Rebecca laughed from her rocking chair and tried to stand.

"Stay, down, Rebecca. I'll come to you." Deborah planted a kiss on Sarah's silky dark hair as she passed. Her niece muttered a greeting but didn't look up from her novel.

Rebecca lowered the few inches she had risen and smiled at Deborah. "Did you have a nice afternoon, Deb?"

Deborah paused. Instead of answering, she held out the paper. "Look what Charlie drew."

Rebecca took the paper in her hands and her eyes widened. "Oh, Deborah! It's simply delightful! He really is gifted, isn't he? I think he captured your vitality so well."

George stood and wiped his brow on his sleeve. He was breathing hard and a big smile lit up his face. He grabbed James under one arm and Susannah under the other. They squealed as he walked towards the women.

"What is simply delightful?" he asked, peering over Rebecca's shoulder.

Rebecca held the paper up and George nodded. "That's our Deborah, alright. He missed that big hairy wart on your nose, but otherwise, it is pretty close."

Deborah swatted his arm but smiled. "It is a good likeness, isn't it?"

"Aye, Deb. You're lovely, lass." He set the children on the floor and they moved by their mother to look at the sketch. George headed towards the door to the shop. "I'll be right back."

William and Sarah joined the others around Rebecca's chair, all excited about the portrait. Sarah declared that posing for a picture was positively the most romantic thing she had ever heard of.

Soon, George returned, setting a carved wooden frame finished in a dark oak stain on the table. He joined the group and took the picture from Rebecca. "I finished this frame last week and was going to put it in the window to sell, but I think this is a better use." He opened the backing and slid Deborah's portrait inside. He turned it around with a flourish and the children clapped.

Deborah crossed to George and took the frame. She squeezed his arm and smiled up at him. "Thanks, George. That was good of you."

George placed the frame on the shelf above the stove. James climbed back on William's back, and Susannah settled on top of Sarah. They started to laugh and squeal as their mounts tried to unmount them. Deborah breathed in the cacophony of this happy little group, feeling their laughter soothe her soul.

Later that evening, a knock sounded at the door. One of the local boys handed George a note. He glanced at the name on the front as he closed the door. "It's for you, Deborah." He pretended like he was breaking the seal as she hopped to her feet.

"Don't you dare, George. Give it to me." She snatched the paper out of his hand and went into her bedroom. She unfolded a piece of paper to show a quick drawing of a donkey with Charlie's face. Under the sketch were the words, "See you in a week. Sorry for showing my true form. Charlie."

Deborah smiled despite the linty irritation that still stuck to her happiness. She folded the paper in half, then half again, tucking it into the top drawer of her bureau.

CHAPTER 10

"You're at the market more frequently, Deborah. Charlie must be back in town. Why don't you invite him over for supper after church tomorrow?" Rebecca's face was deliberate innocence.

The question caught Deborah off guard. Both of their knitting needles stopped in unison, and Deborah set the yellow baby blanket she was knitting in her lap. "Oh, I ran into him a few times last week. He asked how you were feeling." She glanced up at her sister. "I thought that was nice."

"Aye. I feel like one of his whales, but tell him I'm just fine." Rebecca said, setting down a pair of little socks and massaging her belly. "So, do you think he'd like to come to dinner?"

"Oh, I'm sure he'd like to, but he usually goes from Mass

to…spend time with his father. Maybe he could stop by another time. Maybe after the baby." Deborah picked up the blanket again and halfheartedly began knitting.

"Deborah," Rebecca waited until she lifted her eyes to meet hers, "I'd like to know him more. George will behave. We've spoken about it, and I promise he'll be on his best behavior."

Deborah rolled her eyes. "He may try, but you know his eyes give everything away. He can't stand Charlie, and it will be obvious. I'm not interested in putting you in the role of peacemaker. Besides, it's not very serious. He's just a friend."

"Oh please, Deborah. The last two times you've come in from town, you're flushed and disheveled. I know you think I'm a prude, but I know the look of a woman who's just been kissed. Soundly, if my guess is correct."

Deborah knew she was blushing, but she shrugged casually. "I didn't come down in the last shower, Rebecca. I can take care of myself. I'm twenty-six."

"Aye. And unmarried. And under our care." Rebecca flung her knitting in the basket by her chair as her voice rose. "We take that seriously, even if you don't care to."

Deborah stood up, alarmed. She added her knitting to the basket and knelt in front of Rebecca. "Shhh. I'm sorry, Rebecca." She took her hands and kissed them. "Please don't get mad at me. Yes, I do like Charlie. And yes, I've let him kiss me. But I'm careful, I promise. I don't want you upset."

Rebecca's eyes softened, and Deborah squeezed her hand. "Let's just wait until after the baby to put Charlie and George in the same room, shall we?" Deborah said. "Then we can watch the tigers circle each other and see who's strongest."

"George. George is the strongest." Rebecca wagged her eyebrows. "And the most handsome." She smiled now and squeezed Deborah's hand back. "And the most..."

Deborah laughed and stood up, making her way to the stove. "Enough. I know how you feel about George." She tossed a cheeky smile over her shoulder. "That round belly is proof enough."

Rebecca threw a ball of yarn across the room, hitting Deborah in the shoulder. Deborah picked it up, chuckled, and tossed it back in the basket.

"There you are!" Charlie put his cap back on his head and pulled it down over his black curls. Deborah had a sudden desire to snatch it back off and toss it into the street to free those silky waves.

"Aye. Here I am." She took his offered arm, and they steered toward Perth Road. Sunday evening was an unspoken date, and she looked forward to it all week.

Charlie put his hand over hers and tugged her a little

closer. "I dinna ken if the warden would let you out of prison today."

"Just a bit dramatic, aren't we?" Deborah smiled up at him.

"Maybe a little, but every time I think of you being forced to play nursemaid up there, instead of living life down here, it makes my blood boil."

Deborah was quiet for a moment. "Charlie, those little ones are part of me. We've been together since the first. I helped deliver Jamie! I pulled out Sarah's first tooth. William always comes to me with his questions. Susannah wants only me to tuck her in at night. They are my family. No one is making me stay."

"Well, you're where you belong now, love." He smiled at her and tugged her down the cobblestone street. "Where to?"

Deborah wanted to continue the conversation, but the sun was giving off its last few hours of light, and in reality, she did want to take a break. Rebecca was moving slowly this morning and her face was a little swollen. Deborah planned to stay closer to home for Rebecca's delivery, which could be any day now.

"Let's take a long walk down to the Tay. It will be our last one for several days. Rebecca is getting close to giving birth, and I want to stay with her."

Charlie opened his mouth as if to say something, but smiled a thin smile instead. "I've never heard of an unmarried midwife, but I'm sure that Rebecca is glad to have you there."

Deborah laughed. "I didn't take you for the traditional type. Of course unmarried women can be midwives! I've helped deliver twenty-three babies. I'm not quite ready to do it alone, but I am quite capable."

"It just doesn't seem right that someone who hasn't had a baby should deliver other babies."

"Well, what about male doctors? They certainly haven't had babies," Deborah retorted.

"Well, they're...trained," Charlie protested.

Deborah's nostrils flared. "Trained! And what am I?"

Charlie pulled her close and kissed her hair. "Now, don't get all upset. I'm sure you're a right good howdie." He nuzzled behind her ear. "Can we please talk about something else?"

Deborah leaned into him despite herself. Her stomach flipped with his warm breath in her ear, her body betraying her lingering aggravation.

"We can talk about something else. But stop being stupid."

Charlie laughed, pulling back. "Feisty Irishwoman."

"Yes, I am. So be nice." Deborah relaxed a little. She leaned into his arm as they walked along Perth Road for a time, then turned for the harbor. Charlie held her hand at the Bay of Tay, watching the boats bob on the waves.

The footsteps registered in her mind before she heard

them, bringing a sense of alarm and foreboding. When she realized the sound was heading for them, she turned to see William careening around the corner, panting. He bent over and put his hands on his knees when he reached them. "It's time, Aunt Deborah. Da said something about the waters and to find you. Come on." He held out his hand. She let go of Charlie and took hold of William's hand in one motion. She was running before she thought to call back a quick goodnight.

CHAPTER 11

June 12, 1843

Deborah watched Rebecca maul a sheet in her hands, her arms damp with sweat, like the rest of her body. This had been the longest night Deborah could recall. The run home with William seemed like days ago. Lifetimes ago. The thought was sobering, and Deborah once again wondered how Rebecca could be strong for so many hours. She was in excruciating pain, but her labor hadn't progressed. She would drift off to sleep for a couple of minutes, then the pains would wake her again. Caroline Bethune had come, and they both checked, comforted, and massaged Rebecca for over five hours.

But Caroline was called away for a delivery in another part of town. She'd checked Rebecca one last time, then picked up her bag.

She smiled at the panicked look on Deborah's face. "There now. You've enough experience to carry you through. I'll be praying for God's help to be with you, luv. You are ready. You'll know what to do."

"You've delivered over a thousand babies, Caroline! I have only helped with just over twenty. Are you sure you can't stay?" Deborah couldn't begrudge another woman needing a midwife, but she counted on Caroline's wisdom. The older woman just smiled and squeezed her hand before closing the door behind her.

That had been hours ago, and it must be around three in the morning now. Rebecca moaned as she gathered the blanket to her mouth. She leaned down to her sister.

"Dearest, the children are sleeping at Mrs. Carse's. Don't feel that you have to suffer in silence. Yell all you want." Deborah placed her hands over Rebecca's and touched her head to hers until the contraction passed. "Now, take a big breath in, Rebecca." Deborah breathed in with her. "That's good. Now, during the next one, let's breathe like that instead of holding your breath."

"I'll try, Deborah." She took another ragged breath. "Do you think," she hesitated. "Do you think George could come in? I know he's so worried, and I just want to hold on to him through the pains."

Deborah paused, biting her lip. She'd never had a man in the delivery chamber before. It was generally seen as a domain of women, but Rebecca had a point now that they were on their own without Caroline. "I'll ask George, Rebecca. We'll see?"

She rose and closed the door behind her. She'd only have a couple of minutes before the next contraction. George sat in the rocking chair near the fire, leaning over with his hands in his hair. He jumped up at Deborah's entrance.

"What's wrong? What's happened? How is she?" The words tumbled out as he crossed the room in three steps.

Deborah shushed him. "She's fine, but it is wearying her to be in pain for so long."

George looked directly at her. "Why is it taking so long? Tell me straight, Deborah."

"Well, the baby's head is down, which is good, but Rebecca is so petite. I think the baby is large and it is having a hard time descending. It may be several hours yet."

"Please, Deborah. Can I go to her? I need her to know that I'm there."

Deborah nodded and sighed. "She wants you, but I didn't know if you'd want to come in. It can get a little...dramatic. There will be lots of blood, but it is normal. You have to trust me and do what I tell you. If you get fussy or ask too many questions, I'm going to kick you back out to the rocking chair. Do you understand?"

George looked at her, amusement showing through the worry. "So, what I'm hearing is that I can see my own wife in my own house only if you say so, and if you don't like how I behave, you'll send me out to sit on my own backside in my own chair that I made myself. Is that all correct, Deborah? I didn't miss anything?"

Deborah nodded. "Exactly. I just want you to stay right by her and comfort her. Every couple of minutes, the pains will come. When they do, I want you to breathe slowly and deeply. Try to get her to breathe with you. She's holding her breath when it hurts, and I think it's making her body too tense. Please, just trust me and stay up by her head. I'll take care of the rest."

She led George into the room, right as Rebecca seized up with another contraction. Deborah motioned to the other side of the bed.

George hurried to her and sat on the bed, hugging her tight to his chest. She clawed at his shirt with the pain, but Deborah saw her breath lengthen out to match his. He kissed her forehead. "That's good, luv. Just hang on to me, Rebecca."

Deborah checked the baby's progress. "That was perfect. Just keep breathing with the pains. We're going to get this little one here in no time."

They went on like that until the sun began creeping in through the curtains. With George there, Rebecca seemed able to breathe. His shirt was wrinkled and bunched, his eyes bloodshot, but he cooed and sang to Rebecca throughout the long hours of night. Rebecca lost strength with the protracted labor and dropped off into exhaustion as soon as a contraction passed.

Finally, as sounds of morning began filling the streets, Rebecca gave a yell that was surely heard down the block. Deborah adjusted the sheets and checked. "We're almost there! I can feel the baby's head. George, help pull her up and put those pillows behind her." Deborah slid a blanket underneath Rebecca and placed another one at the ready beside her.

"Rebecca, with the next contraction, I want you to push with all your might. I know you are so tired, but you need to push now. Harder each time, until I tell you to wait." Deborah took her sister's hand and looked intently into her eyes. "Can you do that, dearest?"

Rebecca didn't answer, but reached for George, pulling him down next to her. Her voice was a whisper. "Keep your head right next to mine? I can do it if you're..."

A contraction cut her short. She pushed with the pain, again and again. Another 20 minutes passed, and Deborah's brow wrinkled in worry. With each contraction, Rebecca was getting weaker. But then Rebecca gasped. She bore down into the pain, hard and steady.

"That's right, Rebecca! One more just like that!" Deborah supported the little head through the next contraction. "Perfect. Now take a nice slow breath through the next pain. Just grab onto George and match his breath. We want the head and shoulders to come nice and slow.

As the baby slid into the world, a tiny cry filled the room, protesting the rude entrance from warmth to cold. Deborah looked at Rebecca, leaning back in exhaustion, but smiling. Deborah felt tears prick her lids as she set the baby on the awaiting blanket. Another bridge to mortality crossed.

"George, come warm up your little girl while I finish helping Rebecca."

He drew his attention away from Rebecca's face for a moment. "It's a girl?"

"Aye, and she wants everyone to know that she's made her appearance!"

He leaned down to kiss Rebecca's sweat-covered forehead. "Sweet Rebecca, did you hear that? We've another lovely lass."

George left Rebecca's side and came to the baby. He gently rubbed his new daughter with a soft cloth.

Deborah continued to assist Rebecca as her tears flowed in earnest. "Oh, Rebecca! You were just marvelous!" She wrapped the baby tightly in a new blanket and kissed the top of her head. "Welcome to the world, sweet one."

Deborah sniffed back more tears as she handed her into George's waiting arms. "You can take her to her momma when you're ready."

George stared at the bundle for a moment, then placed the package across Rebecca's chest, where the child finally stopped crying. Rebecca's arms were weak, but she set one hand gently on the baby's back.

George sat on the bed and kissed Rebecca's hair. Deborah rose slowly and headed to the washbasin. She looked at the group on the bed and lifted her eyes to heaven.

Thank you, Lord. She couldn't have lasted much longer. It was so close. Thank you.

Around noon, Deborah opened the door slowly, peeking in. "All set for some eager brothers and sisters?" She had waited until after breakfast so Rebecca could get a little sleep, then gathered the Wright children from next door. Around noon, Deborah opened the door slowly, peeking in. "All set for some eager brothers and sisters?" She had waited until after breakfast so Rebecca could get a little sleep, then gathered the Wright children from next door.

Rebecca looked up from the pillows, the baby resting against her chest. She smiled a droopy smile and nodded slowly. "Aye. Let them come in."

Four sets of feet tiptoed into the room and gathered around their mother's bed. "Come meet your little sister."

George woke from the chair in the corner and ran a hand over his face. He looked a mess, but he smiled as Jamie ran into his arms. "Let's see your wee sister, shall we, Jamie?"

Jamie nodded. They approached the little bundle and Rebecca drew back the blankets, showing the soft hair and chubby cheeks of a perfect little girl. She reached her tiny fingers out and flexed them, drawing a chorus of admiration from her proud siblings. The children touched and caressed their little sister.

Sarah bit her lip and sat down by her mother. "Can I hold her yet, Mama?"

"Certainly, love." Rebecca turned to George. "Can you help her?"

Sarah moved towards the chair, and George gently plucked the sleeping baby from Rebecca. He planted a kiss on the soft forehead and moved towards Sarah, beaming in the chair.

Once the baby settled in her arms, Sarah looked up at George. "What are we going to call her?"

George and Rebecca glanced at each other and smiled. Rebecca looked at Deborah. "We thought we'd call her after her kind and courageous aunt who helped her into this world. She's named Deborah, but we'll call her Debbie."

Deborah gasped, tears blurring her vision. She went to Rebecca's bedside and took her hand, kissing it. "Oh, Rebecca!"

"After last night, I don't know any other name that would feel right. She's just meant to be your namesake."

Deborah couldn't stop the tears. She stood and walked to where Debbie had found her sister's finger. Sarah glanced up at Deborah. "Look at how tiny her fingers are, Aunt Deborah!"

"Yes. Isn't she just perfect?" Deborah gently touched the baby's smooth cheek. She looked around the room. Rebecca, worn but radiant. George, proud and joyful. The children, quietly delighted. And tiny Debbie, her precious little namesake, cooed safely in Sarah's arms.

This. This is heaven.

CHAPTER 12

The next weeks were full of more heaven, with plenty of terrestrial moments in between as the family adjusted to the demands of a newborn.

Rebecca wiped an arm across her brow and dropped the letter she'd been writing to her father. She leaned her head back against the rocking chair. Deborah tracked her movements. She placed Debbie in the cradle with a kiss, earning a coo from the six-week-old baby.

She went to Rebecca's side, concerned by the flush on her sister's cheeks. "What's wrong, Rebecca? You don't look well."

Rebecca clutched her head. "Can you help me to bed? I'm suddenly not feeling well. I thought it was just this hot day, but..."

Deborah placed a hand on her sister's cheek and her brow

wrinkled in alarm. "You're burning up!" She turned to Sarah. "Please keep an eye on Debbie, Sarah. Make sure Jamie doesn't hold her again, alright? Your momma isn't feeling very well right now and needs to rest."

Sarah stood and came to her mother. "Are you alright, Momma?"

"I'm sure I will be, dear. I just need to lie down a bit."

Sarah and Deborah exchanged concerned glances at the weakness in Rebecca's voice. "I'll watch the baby, Momma. Don't worry."

Jamie and Susannah continued with their blocks in the corner as Deborah grasped Rebecca's hands and pulled her to her feet. She helped her into the bedroom and out of her heavy brown dress. When Rebecca settled on the bed, Deborah took her hand in hers. She felt for Rebecca's pulse and was alarmed to find it racing. "I know you haven't been back to full strength since the baby, but how long have you been feeling this poorly, Rebecca?"

"I was a little dizzy and tired yesterday, but didn't think much of it. It was just after breakfast today that my head started feeling all muddled and the heat became so intense. My stomach is cramping something terrible. Dearest, please get George for me?"

Deborah nodded and went downstairs. She paused at the entrance to George's shop and rested her head against the wood, giving him one more moment of peace and innocence. The heavy wood creaked as she opened it. She schooled her expression as she turned to him, bent over a chair on his lathe.

He looked up and smiled. "Hello, Deb. What brings you down to the dungeon this morning?"

"George, I think you need to come upstairs. Rebecca's not well."

His cheery expression turned in an instant as he stood and brushed the dust from his apron. "What's wrong, Deborah?" He tossed his apron over the table.

They were already walking towards the door when she finally spoke. "I'm sure she'll be fine, but she's got a sudden fever. She doesn't look well."

He took the stairs two at a time and was by Rebecca's bedside in a moment. He put his hand on her forehead. "Love, you're hotter than August." He reached out for the cool cloth Deborah handed him, soaked from the bedside pitcher. Rebecca moaned softly and put her hands over her abdomen. He lowered his voice. "Deborah, let's get a doctor here. I'd feel better if someone looked at her."

Deborah nodded. "I'll go for Dr. Duncan over on Wyngate. Keep her cool. And don't let the children enter in case it's something catching. I'll see if Sarah can get everyone ready for a walk down to Mary's. I'll be back soon."

After waiting an hour for the doctor to return to his shop, Deborah returned with Alexander Duncan to find Rebecca much worse. The doctor took off his heavy black coat and set down his bag near the bed. He approached Rebecca and gently raised her hand to feel her pulse. He examined her mouth, listened to her heart, and asked a few more questions.

Doctor Duncan gathered his belongings and motioned for George to follow him out of the room. Deborah was close behind, holding baby Debbie. She put the infant down in her cradle by the table and came to stand by George. The tired-looking doctor drew a weathered hand across his cheek.

"What do you think it is, Doctor?" George asked as he followed the elderly man to stand near the window.

"I can't be sure, but the high fever, abdominal pain, headaches, chills, nausea, and racing pulse seem to suggest what we're calling Relapsing Fever. Some are misdiagnosing it as influenza, but Doctor John Cormack in Edinburgh is suggesting this is a whole different disease altogether. Their hospitals are full of it this summer and every house I've been to today is more of the same. We'll have to see how it progresses, watching for white matter on the tongue and tenderness of the liver as the sure signs of what we're dealing with."

George interrupted. "How serious is it? What's the treatment?"

Dr. Duncan shook his head. "I'm afraid it's quite serious. Relapsing Fever is just what it sounds like. After about five days, the fever may break. There could be a full week or even two of improved health, but then we'll watch for it to come again. That's when the fever is most severe, with shaking chills followed by intense sweating, falling body temperature, and low blood pressure."

He ran his hand over his white beard and shook his head. He looked between George and Rebecca. "I wish I had better news, but if it were my own loved one, I'd like the truth. I've seen many people recover, but about 1 in 20 will fail after the fever returns. Rebecca is weak already and hasn't recovered from childbirth. You need to ken that this is a very serious illness, even for those with a hearty constitution. I'd keep the other children out of the room, but the bairn should be protected if Rebecca can continue nursing."

George was silent and stiff. Dr. Duncan turned his attention to Deborah. He set his bag on the table and took out several small bottles, setting them down as he spoke. "Each morning and eve, give her six grains of calomel, twelve of jalap, and one drop oil of peppermint. I'll be by in two days to check on her, but please send a runner if she worsens before that. We'll hope for the best, but if you're a praying soul, some time on your knees is probably as good a medicine as that concoction could ever be."

He snapped his bag closed and smiled sadly. He grasped George's arm and gave it a reassuring squeeze. He turned on his way to the door. "And mind, don't let Paddy O'Neil or any of those other quacks near her. I've nothing against their being Irish, just against their being stupid. O'Neil is telling folk to throw straw under a moving horse at a funeral to cure skin disease or pass a babe with whooping cough under the belly of a donkey. He does more harm than good and keeps people from getting legitimate medical attention."

George nodded. He walked to the coin jar over the stove and removed the doctor's payment, and thanked him as he left. His Adam's apple bobbed up and down as he swallowed hard, then swallowed again.

Deborah took his hand, squeezing it. "Remember, George, no borrowing trouble. We'll take good care of her."

He squeezed her hand back and nodded, still fighting for control. When he finally spoke, his voice was level. "I'll go see to the children. Perhaps Mrs. Carse could keep them safe at her place. Will you stay with Rebecca? And don't tell her..."

"There's nothing to tell yet. We'll wait and see."

Deborah picked up the baby as George left and went to where Rebecca was sleeping. She sat in the rocker, soothing the baby and herself with the rhythmic motion, closing her heart against the possibilities. She squeezed her eyes tight. Rebecca needed her right now, and giving in to tears wouldn't help anyone.

Many people recover. Many people recover.

She rocked the words back and forth in her mind as she stared out into the darkness.

CHAPTER 13

Five days later, George poked his head through the bedroom door. "There's a persistent and untrustworthy whaler down in my shop thinking he needs to see you, Deb."

Deborah rolled her eyes and looked at Rebecca's sleeping form. "Can you stay for a bit? She's stirring."

George nodded. "I'm happy for the break. I wanted to check in on her this afternoon. Go on down."

Deborah tried to smooth the wrinkles out of her dress as she walked downstairs. Charlie looked out of place among the carpenter's tools, his hat in his hands. He smiled sadly when he saw her and gathered her up in his arms in one motion.

"We just got in this morning. I heard about Rebecca from one of your neighbors at the pub. How bad is it?"

Deborah closed her eyes and leaned into his warmth. "It's bad, Charlie. Have you heard of Relapsing Fever?"

Charlie groaned. "I hate to say that I have. We saw it on vessels too many times this summer. They're talking about it all over Dundee. There's not a block without a case. Is the doctor sure?"

Deborah nodded into his chest. "She has all the signs. Fever, abdominal pain, vomiting. Her tongue is covered..." she trailed off. "Anyway, it's been five days and she's hardly eaten more than a few tablespoons a day. She drifts in and out of delirium. And this first episode is supposed to be easier on the patient than the relapses. I don't know if she can handle much more." She squeezed her eyes shut to try to stop the tears.

Charlie kissed the top of her head. "Well, she has the best of nurses." He pulled her closer. "Stay close for a little while, lass. You've too much on your shoulders." He stroked her hair as she cried.

"I don't know what I'd do without her, Charlie. She's more than just my sister or best friend. She's truly been my mother after we lost ours when I was four." Deborah wiped her nose on her sleeve and sniffed. "I can't lose her. I'm so scared."

"Shh, love. Get it all out." He took out a handkerchief and handed it to her, pulling her close. They stayed that way for several minutes, then Deborah lifted her head at the sound of George's shoes on the steps. Charlie ducked his head for a quick kiss, then released her. "I'll leave you to take care of her, but send a note if you need me." He started towards the door, then paused. He turned back to her, rubbing his hand along her cheek. "We'll hope for the best."

The outside door closed as George entered from the back. He looked around the room and exhaled as if relieved. "I'm glad I don't need to chase him off. Rebecca's asking for you, Deborah."

She went up the stairs behind George and into the bedroom. She let out a pent-up breath when she saw Rebecca sitting in bed, propped up by a few pillows. Her cheeks were hollow, but her eyes were open, framed by dark circles.

Deborah hurried to Rebecca's side and placed a hand on her forehead. She bit her lip to stop the tears of relief and anxiety. "Welcome back, sweet sister. You've been a bit lazy the last few days." She stroked her clammy cheek, grateful for the coolness she felt.

"Where are the children? I know I've nursed Debbie a few times, but I haven't heard the others."

Deborah nodded. "The children are over at Mrs. Carse's. We both go there to visit a few times a day. The doctor said Debbie could stay and try to nurse; that it may protect her. We've been giving her goat's milk as well."

Rebecca smiled weakly. "Can you bring everyone home now? The pain is lessened and my head is clear for the first time this week. I don't even know what day it is."

"Thursday." George came around to the other side of the bed and took her hand. "And stay abed as long as you need to." His voice choked with emotion as he squeezed her hand. "I'm so glad to see you sitting up, luv." He looked across the bed at Deborah. "We're so glad you're back."

Rebecca looked between George and Deborah, recognition dawning. "There's more, though."

George's face crumbled. He ran a hand across Rebecca's cheek, lips pressed tight together, emotion flooding his face. He swallowed hard, then abruptly left the room. The stairwell door slammed. The shop door closed. Sounds of a hammer echoed from below.

Rebecca sank down on the pillows, eyes closed. "Tell me."

"Nothing is certain..." Deborah trailed off.

"Tell me, Deborah."

Deborah took a long breath and tipped her head to one side, looking at Rebecca's sunken eyes. She took her sister's hand in her own. "Rebecca, you likely have Relapsing Fever. Dr. Duncan is sure of it. It's all over Dundee and clear down to Edinburgh. You pulled through the first round of fever. You may feel well for a week or even two, then the fever will probably come back again." Deborah was silent.

"Tell me all of it." Rebecca listened, motionless on the bed.

Deborah swallowed hard. "When the fever returns, it will probably be worse the second time around. Some people have died." Deborah rushed to finish. "But many, many live and recover fully. That's what's going to happen, Rebecca. We'll take good care of you."

Rebecca nodded, her eyes still closed. "Well, then." A tear dangled on her long lashes. She squeezed her eyes tighter and it dropped down her cheek. After a moment of silence, she fluttered them open and turned towards Deborah. "I'd like to go out to the kitchen, Deb. Can you make me a bed on the couch? I'll not stay in this room until," she paused, "until I have to."

Deborah bit the inside of her cheek to control the emotion building up. "Of course, Rebecca. I'll get it ready for you and George can lift you out when he returns."

Rebecca's composure collapsed, and a sob escaped her frail body. "Oh, poor, poor George." She turned her head to the wall and pulled the covers to her face, her quiet sobs filling the room.

Deborah stood and closed the door behind her, leaning against it for support. She raised her eyes and sent a simple plea heavenward.

CHAPTER 14

A few days later, Deborah crossed to where Rebecca lay on the couch. Before Rebecca saw her and softened her expression, Deborah saw the weariness written on her face. "How about trying some more soup?" she asked, pulling a chair next to the bed with a simmering bowl. "It's not as good as yours, but everyone gobbled it up at dinner."

"That would be nice. Thanks."

Rebecca sat up as Deborah lifted the spoon to her mouth and held her breath while she sipped the warm liquid, willing it to strengthen, to heal. What else could she do? Rebecca sipped three more spoonfuls, then the pain lines returned. "That was good, Deb. I think I'll try a little more later."

"Please, Rebecca. You need more." Deborah tried to not sound desperate, but she knew she was pleading. "You've got to get more in your body. I won't let you keep nursing Debbie if you can't get more food down."

"Sweet Deborah." Rebecca reached out to stroke her sister's dark hair, twirling it around her finger. "How can I help you understand? Nursing her is my last gift. My last blessing." She paused, then sat up, determination mixed with the pain she felt at the effort. "Will you tell her that someday? Tell her that feeding her was a balm to my heart at the end."

"Stop it!" Deborah pulled away from Rebecca. "Stop talking that way! You aren't going anywhere. I can tell you are getting stronger every day! It has been days since you've been fevered."

Rebecca placed her hand gently on Deborah's head. She spoke with a strength that belied her pale face and sunken cheeks. "Deborah, dearest. I need you. I need to talk to someone about the fact that I am going to die."

Deborah started to say something, but Rebecca continued. "I can't talk to George; he won't hear anything of it. But you know I am not getting better. I barely made it through Debbie's birth and the last round of fever. This last week has been such a gift. Spending time with the children, enjoying the sunshine. But even without the fever, I feel," she paused as she searched for words. "I feel life slipping out of me." Tears welled up in her eyes and fell down her cheeks, but her gaze was direct and filled with strength.

"But you may get better," Deborah interrupted, willing herself not to cry. "The doctor said it was a miracle you survived Debbie's birth, then you pulled so well through the fevers. You'll just keep on resting until your body finishes healing. I can do everything! You don't have to lift a finger until you are stronger."

Rebecca smiled, even though the tears kept falling. "I already don't lift a finger, as you well know." She paused and looked directly at Deborah. "Deborah, when I woke up yesterday, the sun shone so warmly on my face and it felt like heaven was just outside the window. I don't know how to explain it, except to say that I know that my time is coming. Sometimes, I feel such comfort in it, then I feel a sense of panic about having to leave all of you." Rebecca choked back tears.

Deborah opened her mouth to speak, but Rebecca held up her hand, her voice rising. "I am dying!" She grabbed Deborah's arm. "Please don't make me do it alone. I need you!"

The sobs took over now, as Deborah enclosed Rebecca in her arms and wept.

After a moment, Deborah found her voice again. "Rebecca," Deborah said, her voice a whisper, "I will try to the very end to get you better, but I've never doubted your inspiration." She kissed the top of her head and rested her wet cheek against the silky blonde locks. "Sweet sister, I will help you leave."

The sun bent long rays through the trees where the Wright children were climbing. William turned upside down, his knees anchoring him to a large branch. He beat his chest and screeched.

Rebecca laughed quietly. "I'm glad we brought the monkeys out today, Deb. They are so happy."

Deborah nodded and smiled, but her voice stuck in her throat, caught on the grief of this perfect day. The last few days, Rebecca had been getting up more and more, but her movements were slow and her face had a gray cast to it.

Deborah had dipped into her meager savings to hire this ride into the countryside, but didn't regret it. Rebecca looked so content lying on Deborah's lap, two-month-old Debbie swaddled beside her. She sucked her fist, a sure sign she wouldn't be sleeping for much longer. Deborah looped one of Rebecca's curls around her finger and admired the way it shone in the sun. She let it run through her fingers and fall across her lap. Rebecca's simple cotton dress hung on a body leaving, ounce by ounce.

Deborah saw tears pooling in her sister's eyes. "What is it, Rebecca? Are you hurting again? Here, hand me Debbie, and let's get you home.

"No. I'm fine, Deb. I don't want to go anywhere. It's just so...perfect." She squeezed her eyes shut against the tears.

Deborah bit down hard on her lip. When she trusted herself to speak, she tried to keep her tone light. "Well, then we'll just have to stay out here until dark so we can gather as much happiness as we can..." Her voice trailed off.

"I'd like that," Rebecca responded, her voice breaking on the words.

They spent a moment in silence, Deborah stroking her sister's hair, Rebecca stroking the baby's sleeping face. Rebecca turned to look up at Deborah, the sunset framing her face with gold. "Your strength is my one consolation, Deborah. The children will need so much comfort. I know you'll be able to love them while George...," She took a shaky breath. "While George grieves. He's lost so much, and he...," she swallowed until she could speak. Her voice escaped in a whisper. "He loves me so."

Her body shook with an oppressed sob, and little Debbie let out a wail as Rebecca wiped at her tears. Rebecca shushed her as she uncovered her breast and drew the baby close. Soon, the cries were stilled and replaced by Debbie's content sucking.

Deborah watched the pair, perfect together in the dusky light. She didn't bother with the tears that fell down her cheeks and landed in Rebecca's curls. The ache in her heart was such a sharp contrast to the late summer sun filtering through the leaves and the children's laughter filling the air. Deborah closed her eyes, soaking it up with all her senses, canning the moment in glass to bring out in winter.

She'd read that hurricanes had a calm center; a moment of peace before the winds tore everything apart again. They were in that center now, safe in the storm's eye. But Deborah knew a hurricane was just around the corner, and Rebecca looked weak enough to blow away on the breeze.

The next morning, George quietly came out of the bedroom he shared with Rebecca. He sat at the table and buried his head in his arms. Deborah turned off the stove and hurried to his side.

"What is it?"

He looked at her, all present and past griefs pooling in his eyes. "She's fevered again, Deborah. And I can't wake her."

CHAPTER 15

SEPTEMBER 2, 1843

Deborah raised her head with a start. *How had she fallen asleep?* The room was quiet in the dark of night, a small lamp casting a low glow over the still form in the bed. She exhaled when she saw the labored rise and fall of Rebecca's chest. George's head rested on the bed, Rebecca's hand in his own as he sat on the floor. He raised bloodshot eyes to meet hers.

"Is she...," Deborah whispered.

"She's still here, poor thing. She's still here." George rubbed Rebecca's hand and brought it to his lips. His voice caught. "But not for much longer, I think."

Rebecca turned at the sound of his voice. She brought her hand weakly to his head and ran her hand slowly through his hair. "Sleep, George. I want Deborah." He began to protest, but she lifted a finger to his lips. "I'm not going anywhere just yet. Sleep, luv."

George reluctantly squeezed her hand and left the room, looking backward over his shoulder. "Deborah, come get me in one hour." She nodded and moved her chair closer to Rebecca. She removed the wet cloth and finger-combed back the silken hair that was matted on her forehead. She turned to dip the cloth in the basin and wrung the water almost dry. She lay the wet cloth on Rebecca's burning brow and forced a smile. "How does that feel, Rebecca? Do you think you could drink a little?"

Rebecca smiled weakly up at her sister and tried to raise herself on the pillow. "No. I just need you right now." Deborah propped another pillow behind Rebecca and took her hand again.

"Isn't there anything you need? Let me be useful, dear one."

Rebecca tried to squeeze her hand. "I'm so glad you are here."

Each word seemed a slow leak to her strength. Deborah shushed her. "Let's talk later. You need to rest now."

Rebecca continued, even though the effort was obviously taxing her. "I need you to promise."

"What do you need me to promise, Rebecca? You know I'll do anything for you. Anything."

Rebecca took a hoarse breath. She looked at Deborah with strength and conviction that didn't seem possible from her weak and fragile frame. "I need you to be my children's mother."

"Oh, Rebecca!" Deborah kissed her hand. "You know I will! I will always be there for them until even little Debbie is all grown up and married. I couldn't love them more if they were mine. I promise that I will make you so very proud of them." Her voice trailed off as she choked back a sob.

"I know. I know you will. But that's not the promise." She reached to take out her small gold earrings, but her arm failed halfway, dropping back on the quilt. "My earrings. Help me."

Deborah helped pull the backing from the small gold orbs. She moved to put them on the bedside table next to the basin, but Rebecca motioned for her to stop. "They're yours."

"Rebecca, no. These were a wedding present from George."

Rebecca ignored her and struggled to pull the wedding ring off her left hand, though it hung loosely on her finger. The gold band seemed to weigh her fragile hand down to the bed, but she lifted her arm and placed the ring into Deborah's hand with the earrings. She closed her hand around Deborah's and sighed. She leaned back further into the pillows, her voice diminished to a whisper.

"I give you everything I have. Everything. They are yours now." She looked up into Deborah's eyes with an intensity that belied her frail body.

"Dearest, I want you to promise me you'll marry George after I'm gone."

Deborah gasped, but Rebecca continued, her voice getting stronger. "My children need a mother, and George needs a wife. You need a husband. You all need each other. It's how it's supposed to be." She looked hard and steadfastly into Deborah's eyes. Her hand squeezed around Deborah's until the earrings poked into her skin. "Promise me."

Deborah stared silently at Rebecca, her mouth open in shock. The gold ring seemed made of fire in her hand. She couldn't recall anything that Rebecca had ever asked of her. Demanded of her. Deborah took a long and low breath and kissed the top of Rebecca's head like she had been kissed so many times by her as a child. Always loving. Always serving. What Rebecca needed most right now was peace about the future. To know those she loved would be loved still. Deborah knew she would do anything to help Rebecca on her final journey. Anything to repay her sister for a life of love. Anything.

Even lie.

"I promise, Rebecca. I promise."

Rebecca sighed and collapsed deeper into the pillows. She closed her eyes. Her face, though contorted with pain, took on an otherworldly glow. There was even a small smile on her lips. Deborah clenched the jewelry in her hand and held Rebecca's with the other. She sat straight in the chair, her hand tight around Rebecca's earthly treasures. She looked at the wall as tears rolled down her cheeks.

Rebecca's whispered goodbyes were barely discernible, but she smiled softly as her children kissed her, one by one. Deborah ushered them out and shut the door behind them as the sun began to creep into the room. They all turned towards her, like a wound closing in on itself. Deborah held them in their grief as they sat on the floor, sobbing. She wanted to speak comfort to them, tell them of angels and heaven and God. But she couldn't get any words past her sorrow. Somehow, they all eventually stood up and she found shoes and bonnets and hats for equal parts feet and heads. She wrapped Debbie tightly and set her in Sarah's arms, sending them out the door for Mary Carse's. She leaned against the closed door, trying to breathe in a measure of control.

When her breaths came normally again, she opened the bedroom door and crept to Rebecca's bed. George had been there for hours, holding Rebecca's hand and singing quietly. His hair drooped in his eyes, and whiskers covered his face in three days of grief. She knew Rebecca was conscious for part of the night, but Deborah left George alone with his precious wife.

He had opened the door at sunrise and asked her to wake the children to come to say goodbye. Now, as she met his eyes across their shared love, she saw the raw despair there and knew it was almost over. George's song melted away as Rebecca's breath paused like a tide suspended before a labored release.

Deborah choked back her tears and sat on the right of Rebecca's bed, taking Rebecca's hand in her own. "Let's sing her home, George."

He nodded and inhaled, taking Rebecca's other hand in his own. His voice was quiet but sure as he joined Deborah.

We two have run about the slopes,
and picked the daisies fine;
But we've wandered many a weary foot,
Since good old times.
We two have paddled in the stream,
from morning sun till dine;
But seas between us broad have roared
Since good old times.
And there's a hand my trusty friend!
And give a hand o' thine!
For good old times.

Her voice faded away as Rebecca suddenly took a breath, gasping in what was left of the world for her, and sank into the bed. Deborah and George's eyes flew up to each other in unison, then down to Rebecca. They watched for another breath as they held their own. When the stillness settled, they knew.

The peace came first. It felt almost like a bit of heaven falling around them with the reassurance that this ending was not the end. Deborah closed her eyes and let it surround her for a moment, holding Rebecca's limp hand. Bridging the moment between heaven and earth.

Then the grief crashed on her in a wave. Deborah kissed Rebecca's peaceful face, choking on the emotion seizing her chest. She stumbled out of the room as George clawed at the blanket, burying his sobs in the folds. Deborah closed the door to his grief, falling into the sofa and pressing a pillow tightly against the hollow place in her middle. The tears choked through and burned into the fabric, as she mourned the loss of the most precious person in her life. Mother. Sister. Friend.

She heard George's cries through the door. She should go to him and say something comforting. She should write to Da and all the family in Ireland. She should go help the children understand and mourn. But she simply pulled the pillow closer and curled up with her pain.

I'll find strength for all of them tomorrow. Tonight, the grief is all mine.

CHAPTER 16

The funeral was short and the crowd was small at Howff Cemetery. A few of the shopkeepers from their street came to pay their respects, and Mary Carse was in the middle of the Wright children, handing out handkerchiefs and snuggling them into her softness. Though Deborah had written, she knew her da couldn't make the journey. The rest of those who would miss Rebecca mourned from Ireland.

The ivy-covered tombstones were as comforting as Reverend James Ewing's formal message about the glorious afterlife. His words blended into the moss of the ancient place, already witness to centuries of pain. All Deborah could think about was this life. These children. This sleeping baby in her arms. This grieving man at her side. She could barely stand upright in her pain, but she knew they needed her. Thinking of Rebecca brought her strength. It must have been so hard for a girl of fourteen to take on the role of mother, even as she grieved her own. But that's what Rebecca had done so beautifully, and what Deborah would do now.

She glanced at George. He hadn't said more than a few words since Rebecca's passing two days ago. His eyes were swollen and his face was ruddy from the constant tears.

Deborah remembered asking him all those years ago in the orchard if he truly loved Rebecca. She had never doubted his feelings since then. Watching him gaze at Rebecca across a room. Watching him serve her. But watching him let her go opened Deborah's eyes to just how much he adored her, and what this loss would cost him. She'd heard his sobs from downstairs as he labored straight through two nights to make Rebecca's coffin. His last gift.

She shifted Debbie to her other arm and squeezed George's arm. He turned to her and nodded, but his blank expression didn't change.

A motion by the side of the gate caught her eye, and she noticed Charlie standing by the church behind an ivy-covered gate. He nodded to her and patted his heart.

After the service, they all walked home. The September sunshine broke through the morning haze and seemed to mock the gloomy mood of the group dressed in black as they walked back to Bucklemaker Wynd. A few people stopped and nodded as they passed, remembering their own walks back home. Their losses. Somehow, she found more comfort in their brief acknowledgment than in Reverend Ewing's entire sermon.

They went first to Mary Carse's small apartment, where she had a lovely lunch set out for them. Cock-a-leekie soup steamed from a cast iron pot, and fresh oatcakes sat on the table, covered with a large white tea towel. She set an overflowing dish of cranachan in the center of the table, the fluffy cream and bright strawberries stark against the mood in the room. Mary bustled about, filling plates and kissing foreheads. She took Debbie and prepared the goat's milk bottle from Deborah's bag.

With the baby enclosed against Mary's chest, drinking from the bottle, and the children settled with their steaming bowls, Deborah took a sip of her soup. *Had she eaten today? Did she yesterday?* The liquid was warm and soothing down her throat, but somehow brought the tears back to her eyes. She looked up to see George staring at his bowl as if willing it to his mouth. Willing himself to want to eat. To want to live.

Deborah took a deep breath and shook the tears out of her eyes. "Mrs. Carse, this is just lovely. You are too kind." She took a large bite of bread and looked at George. "Isn't cock-a-leekie your new favorite soup, George?"

George's habitual manners kicked in and he pulled the spoon to his mouth. "It is a wonderful meal and such a kind gesture, Mrs. Carse. Thank you for your goodness to my family." He took another bite, and Deborah relaxed a little.

They would figure this out. They would keep eating. And somehow, they'd keep living.

Two weeks later, Deborah sat in the rocking chair, baby Debbie's warmth against her neck. She set the bottle down on the small table, drew the little bundle over her shoulder, and rested her head against the baby's curls. Soft and blonde. So like Rebecca's.

You'll miss so much, love. But I'll try. I promise.

She patted Debbie's back, then settled her on her lap. She nibbled at her chubby feet and Debbie rewarded her with a toothless grin and a shriek. "Oh! You like that, little lady?" She traced a creeping spider up her legs to wiggle under her armpits. Debbie grinned and giggled.

Jamie came over from playing with his wooden blocks and held onto the side of the rocking chair. It was quiet in the house, with Susannah playing in a corner with her rag dolls and William and Sarah returning to Burgh School earlier that week.

"Remember how to play peek-a-boo, Jamie?"

The toddler nodded. "If I lay Debbie on the blanket, do you want to try to make her laugh?"

He nodded again, so she arranged the blanket on the rough-hewn timber floor. Debbie smiled at her brother. He put his hands in front of his face, then peeked out, earning a sweet giggle.

"That's right, Jamie." Deborah squeezed him close. "See how she loves you, big brother? Can you play for a few more minutes while I check the stove?"

Jamie nodded and turned back to his baby sister. Deborah was most worried about Jamie since Rebecca's passing. He had hardly said a word since the funeral. She'd have to involve him more with caring for the baby since Debbie had a way of bringing out smiles from everyone.

She stood and looked out the window at the usual morning haze. She'd put off going to the market for as long as she could, but she'd have to bundle everyone up and go today even though the October weather had turned cooler. They'd used up all the pantry supplies and the food neighbors had kindly brought by, though Mrs. Carse continued bringing fresh goat milk for Debbie. The last of the potatoes simmered on the stove for lunch.

She gathered the children's shoes and was looking for the simple sling she carried Debbie in when George came upstairs.

"Where are you off to?" he asked, brushing a few specks of sawdust off his shirt onto the landing before coming inside.

"Just a trip to the Greenmarket. We're out of everything."

"If you want to leave the children, I'll eat my lunch now."

He walked to Debbie and Jamie on the floor, pulling Jamie onto his lap.

Deborah sighed thankfully. "That would be wonderful, George. I haven't done a trip with all of them yet without..."

"I know. I've got them. You go ahead."

Deborah wrapped her heavy shawl around her shoulders and picked up her woven basket. "I won't be long."

The heavy air and overcast sky that greeted her seemed fitting. She made her way over to the Greenmarket and filled her basket with vegetables and a sack of oats. Deborah turned away from the stall and saw Charlie walking towards her. She quickened her pace and met him partway.

"Well, hello, lovely lass." He reached for her hand and pulled her behind a sweets booth in one motion. He looked her over. "How are you, dearie?" he asked, gliding his hands down her arms.

The touch was refreshing. "A little better. The children are back in school, and they seem to be adjusting. Debbie was fussy for a few days getting used to a bottle, but she's calmed down now. Sarah and William have been a big help, but Jamie seems to have the hardest time. I'm not sure it's normal for a boy that age to..."

Charlie interrupted. "No, dear, how are *you*?" He took the basket from her hand and placed it on the ground.

Deborah paused. "A little better each day." She wrapped her arms around her middle. "But there's a big hole inside. I didn't know it could hurt so much."

Charlie pulled her closer and kissed the top of her head. "That's what time is for, love. You'll see." He gathered her up into his arms and stroked her back. "Do you feel like taking a walk?"

"I couldn't possibly, Charlie. George is taking a break from his work while I shop."

He frowned.

Deborah continued in a hurry. "But come with me to the baker's stall? Then the butcher on the way back home?"

"How nice that George could take a break to watch his children." Charlie's voice pinched.

Deborah took a long breath. "Please don't start, Charlie. Not today."

Charlie's face softened. "I'm sorry, love. You're right. I'll be right glad to walk you to the bakers."

It felt good to hold on to his arm, her basket in his other hand. She lay her head against his strong muscles for a moment as they waited for people to pass so they could continue across the square. "That's right, Deborah. Just hang on. I've got you."

The tenderness in his voice brought tears to hover on her lashes, but she blinked them back. She bought the loaves, then led him to Tomlinson's Butcher shop on Hilltown. She made her purchases in silence, then turned to face him as they exited.

"I truly have to go now."

"I ken. You still need some time." He paused and handed

her back her basket. "There wasn't a more devoted sister, Deb. I ken you loved her. But she's gone, and it is time for you to come back to life. To come back to me. She would want you to be happy."

She answered with a hand wiped across her eyes.

"Promise you'll come to the Saturday dance next week. It's time to get out of the house. We'll just stay for a bit, then I'll walk you home. Promise me."

Deborah didn't trust herself to speak with the sudden rush of emotion, so she only nodded.

Charlie looked up and down the street, then planted a quick but firm kiss on her mouth.

"Until next Saturday."

CHAPTER 17

The door swung on its hinges, marking the rapid departure of the children after dinner. Deborah saw George watching her across the table, thoughtfully. She brightened her face and stood. "Can I take your dish over for you?"

"I've got it." George stood and walked to the basin and paused as she joined him there. "How are you, Deb?" he asked, laying a hand on her shoulder and bending his face to look level into her eyes. "You haven't left the house in days, not even for a Sunday stroll."

She tried a smile. "I may go out on Saturday, but it just feels too soon."

He tipped his head, inviting more. When none came, he patted her arm. "I know you are holding us all together, but how are you? Really?"

"Same as you. Trying." She went back to the table and sat, pushing the letter from her da to the center and resting her head in her hands. "It's been two months, but I feel mad at everyone for bustling 'round like normal. It seems the world thinks it can go about its merry way without Rebecca."

"I like to hear you say her name." He took a breath and followed her to the table. "I feel mad every time I hear someone laugh, even the children. Isn't that awful? It doesn't seem right that anyone else can find something to be happy about. I want to shout out at them, 'Don't you know she's gone?'" His voice crumbled, and he leaned on the back of the chair where Rebecca usually sat.

She saw the chair shake as sobs erupted from deep inside his chest. Sharing air with such emotion, she couldn't hold back her own tears. She stood and reached out to him. He came into her arms and lay his head on the top of her head, soaking her hair with his tears.

They stayed that way for several minutes, living in the freshness of the pain until space came between the sobbing, then sobbing came between the space. George finally pulled away. Deborah wiped a sleeve across her nose, and he handed her a handkerchief.

"What a mess we are," she said, blowing her nose and pocketing the cloth.

He took a deep breath. "Speak for yourself, lass. I hope I don't look near as awful as you." He tried a smile, but it didn't reach his eyes.

"You look worse. But somehow my heart feels a little lighter." She looked up at him, eyes puffy and earnest. "I'm so glad you loved her, too, George. I don't know why that makes it easier, but it does."

He nodded, then pulled her into a hug, resting his chin on the top of her head.

The door swung open again and Sarah, William, and Susannah tumbled in. Following behind William was twelve-year-old Sammy McDougal, who stopped on the threshold, taking in the couple standing by the chairs.

Deborah pulled away from George and smoothed a hand through her hair. "Hello, Sammy. Come on in and close the door." Deborah pushed the chairs in and started towards the cradle.

Sammy had indecision written all over his face, then turned and ran down the stairs.

Susannah took in her father's red face. "Are you missing Momma?"

George nodded his head and sat down on the hearth, pulling her onto his lap. He kissed her hair. "Aye, lass. I miss her fiercely. But do you know what helps?"

"What?"

"Holding a little girl with her mother's sweet goodness. That's what helps me. What helps you when you are missing her?"

"I like hugs from Aunt Deborah. She smells like Momma."

Deborah looked at them from across the room where she was picking up little Debbie, just waking up from a nap. She felt more fatigue than pain now, although her eyes still burned. She walked to where the pair sat.

"Well, I'll never *be* as good as your momma, so I'm glad at least that I can *smell* as good as your momma." She smiled a little and sat beside them on the cold brick. Debbie reached for George, who took her in his arms. He smiled up at Deborah, gratitude in his eyes. She nodded, understanding.

I'll keep living if you will.

Sarah walked over and sat on the floor in front of Deborah, her head resting on her aunt's lap. Deborah stroked her hair, feeling her heart calm with the simple motion.

"And how are you, luv?" She asked her niece.

Sarah shrugged. "Most of the time I'm well enough. But I still expect to see Momma when I come home. I think of things I want to tell her, then it feels like all my insides hurt when I remember that she's..."

Deborah bent down to kiss Sarah's head. "I know, dear. I know."

Sarah coughed and wiped a few tears from her eyes. She coughed again, with more force.

George and Deborah looked at each other with mirrored concern.

"Are you well, lass?" George asked as Deborah's hand came to her niece's forehead.

"Sarah, you're warm."

She snuggled deeper into Deborah's lap. "My head started hurting after dinner, but I thought it was just because I was racing William to Sammy's." She coughed again.

Deborah rose, pulling Sarah with her. "Well, let's get you into your nightgown and to bed a little early. We'll see if you're well enough for school in the morning. Come."

Sarah let herself be led to the bedroom, George's concerned eyes following them.

William came in alone from school the next day, plopping his pile of books by the entrance.

"How's Sarah?"

Deborah picked up her cup. "Her cough is getting worse, but I'm sure she'll be just fine, William. How was school? Are you glad it's Friday?"

William silently sat down at the table. "Aunt Deborah, what's a brazen woman living in a den of sin?" He asked right as Deborah took a drink of water. The liquid caught in her throat and she sputtered to clear the cough.

"Where in the world did you hear that, Will?" She asked the question as she pulled her mouth into a solemn frown and joined him at the table. Knowing she shouldn't be smiling. Knowing she shouldn't want to laugh at those words coming from one so sweet and young.

How would Rebecca handle this?

"Just tell me straight, Aunt Deborah." His face was earnest. "What is a brazen woman?"

She straightened her apron and sat down at the table, facing him, trying to look maternal. "A 'brazen woman' would be someone who doesn't follow God where men are concerned, and a 'den of sin' would be the place where she...," she paused, "doesn't follow God."

William's eyebrows knitted together and he bit his lower lip. Deborah came across the table and lay a hand on his arm as she sat beside him. "Will, what's wrong? Where did you hear a phrase like that?"

She saw big tears pool in his eyes. "Oh, Aunt Deb! You aren't a brazen woman at all!"

She stiffened. "No. I'm not a brazen woman. I try to do my best to follow God." She paused, checking that her face was neutral and reassuring. "But why do you ask?"

"Sammy told me that his mother said you were a brazen woman living in a den of sin and that he wasn't to play with me anymore so as not to be tarnished. Sammy is a cheater at ball anyway and says that Irish people don't wash their hands, so I don't care. I told him so. But I don't want him to call you names. You are the funnest and sweetest auntie anyway, even if his mother thinks you live in a den of sin."

Deborah felt her heart constrict and wrapped her arms

around William. She took a deep breath to control her voice, trying to remember what her sweet sister would've said in such a situation.

Sorry, Rebecca.

"That's alright, Will. Who wants to play with Sammy anyway? He'd poke a hole in your head with those ugly buck teeth of his if he ran into you. He looks like a walrus."

William giggled, even as he wiped a hand across his eyes. "That's right. And he smells bad, too."

"He certainly does. He might not like me, but at least I don't have hair the color of the bottom of the wash barrel."

"Or more freckles than a giraffe."

"Or no more sense than a stone to think he can insult your auntie." She made a show of rolling up her sleeves and putting up her fists. "Do you think I should call him out of his house and insist on fighting him for his insults?"

Now William was really laughing. "I think you should. Everyone would come and watch you wrestle him and rub his big buck teeth in the mud."

"Then I'd kick him in the pants clear out of town until I could push him into Bannerman's pigpen. Maybe he would smell better after that." She pulled him close. "Then he'd know not to mess with the Wright family, wouldn't he?" She planted a big, smacking kiss on his forehead. He promptly rubbed it off with his hand, but he smiled a lopsided grin.

"I love you, Aunt Deborah. We'll let him off the hook for now, but if he says anything again, you can fight him."

"He's lucky this time, but I'll be ready. In the meantime, let's not tell your da what Sammy said, shall we?" William nodded gravely, understanding.

Sarah coughed in the bedroom and Deborah left William at the table, worries about rumors cached under deeper concerns.

CHAPTER 18

Deborah looked outside at the changing colors of the Saturday sky, lighting up in shades of red and purple. The last few days had been tiring but healing in a way. As Sarah grew, she didn't seek affection as much as when she was young. But when she was ill, it was always Aunt Deborah she'd asked for. Deborah looked at her sleeping niece and smiled. She was growing into a beautiful young lady, but asleep, she was the same little girl.

Deborah knew Charlie was probably already waiting for her with the sunset at the corner, and she knew she wasn't going to the dance with him. George was a gentle father, but Sarah needed a mother.

She needs her mother. Deborah blinked back the threatening tears. *But she's only got me. So, I'll stay.*

Deborah closed her eyes for a moment, thinking of how nice it would be to feel Charlie's arms around her. There were times she longed to know him deeper, to talk about what was most important in her heart, but tonight she'd settle for his laugh and a kiss or two.

Instead, she dipped the cloth in the basin next to the bed and wrung out the water. She lay it across Sarah's forehead and caught a drip heading for her ear with her finger. Deborah leaned her head against the back of the chair and inhaled. Sarah would be fine. The herb poultice on her chest seemed to help her breath better, and the fever was almost gone. But Deborah knew how quickly chest congestion could worsen. She knew what to watch for.

Another night. He'll understand.

She picked up a scrap of paper, penned a short note, and sent William to the corner.

⚜⚜⚜

On Sunday evening, Deborah waited outside for her usual stroll with Charlie. Her heart beat erratically and she tried to calm her breathing. She knew he's be disappointed she hadn't shown up on Saturday, but wanted to get the conversation over with and move on. She heard footsteps coming around the corner and watched for him to appear. It was two men she vaguely recognized from the docks. They smiled and nodded as they passed. When they were further down the road, she heard muffled laughter as one glanced back at her.

An arm-linked couple, obviously heading for Perth Road, came on her left. She might be mistaken, but the woman seemed to raise one eyebrow before she straightened her gaze and passed without a greeting. Deborah watched them continue down the walk and saw her gloved hand reach up to the ear of her escort, whispering.

She suddenly felt very exposed standing outside. Charlie would have to come knock. His voice surprised her, and she started.

"Where were you?"

Deborah caught her breath. She couldn't decide if there was more concern or anger in Charlie's voice.

"Good to see you, too," she responded, wrapping her shawl around her against the nip in the air. "I'm doing well. Thanks so much for asking."

Charlie's eyes flashed at the sarcasm. "Where were you? I waited for almost an hour on the corner, looking like a truant schoolboy with nowhere to go. I would've come to the house, but I saw George was home and didn't feel like getting in a fight with a man in mourning." His fists clenched like he very much would like to get into a fight with anyone, mourning or not. "Why didn't you come?"

Deborah matched his gaze, taking a deep breath. "I'm sure that was awkward standing on the corner, but I sent a note. I didn't think you'd been waiting long. Sarah came home from school with a cough on Friday. I've been by her side constantly, replacing the poultices until the phlegm finally broke up this morning. She's doing much better now, but she'll probably still cough for most of this week. It gets worse when she's active, so we're trying to keep her...."

"You aren't her mother," he said, cutting her off and taking hold of her arm, hard.

Deborah's eyes registered shock at his insensitivity. "Pardon me?"

"You aren't her mother, Deborah. You are just an aunt. Tell me, what was her da doing while you were mopping her brow instead of dancing with me? Playing checkers by the fire?"

Her eyes flashed, but she tried to keep her voice steady. "George was taking care of the other children, Charlie. Sarah needed me. You wanted me, but she needed me. I wasn't going to leave her lying ill to go dancing."

He let go of her arm as he let out a stream of air from his lips and ran his hand across the stubble on his face. "Well, maybe I'm tired of getting your leftovers, Deb."

"Really, Charlie? Really?" She turned away, wrapping her arms around her middle.

"Deborah, I ken you felt like you had to take care of Rebecca, but she's gone now. George needs to figure this out on his own. You aren't doing him any favors by providing free labor and letting him shirk his duties. If he can make five children, he can figure out how to care for them without taking advantage of people."

She started to protest, but he cut her off, grabbing one of her shoulders. She stiffened under his touch but closed her mouth.

"Listen, I don't even want to bring this up, but people are gossiping about you living alone with him. I can't believe that I'm having to tell you what is proper, but you have to ken that it looks suspicious, Deb. Your name is being tossed around at the pub, saying you've been warming his bed nice and toasty, even before your sister was gone. You need to make other plans and get out from under his roof. Soon."

"You can't be serious! I'm not abandoning them because drunks have nothing better to do with their time than gossip. The baby is barely three months old, Charlie! What is that poor man supposed to do? How is he supposed to work and support everyone if I'm not there? Do I take Sarah out of school? She's helpful, but she's only thirteen. Thirteen, Charlie! She's still just a little girl. She needs me. They all do." The tears that she'd been holding back started sliding down her cheeks. She brisked them away, shrugging off his hand. "And you're hurting me!"

Charlie took a deep breath. "This isn't going right." He released his hand and ran it through his hair, leaving it tousled like a small boy. Even in her indignation, she had the urge to run her fingers through the silky mass. She hugged the shawl tighter to keep her errant hands confined and met his gaze.

"Hear me out?"

Deborah nodded, pulling out her handkerchief.

"At the dance, I wanted to ask you a question, so that's why I was so mad you didn't show up. I'm going to Mearns, just outside Glasgow, to work in Hazelden Mill bleach works. There's no more whaling until Spring, and I don't want to leave you that long anyway. There's good work down there. They pay fair, and they are hiring women in the print works. They provide separate men's and women's housing, so it's all prim and proper, too. It's a chance to get your own life back, lass. I'm leaving in two weeks on Saturday, and I want you to come with me."

He wiped a tear from her cheek and slid a finger along her neck. "It's time to start fresh, Deborah. Come to Mearns." His voice lowered, and he took a step closer, toying with the curl peeking out of her bonnet. "Maybe, eventually, we'll get married and put down roots there. I want you with me, Deb. Come."

Her response was slow in forming, and he interrupted with a finger on her mouth. He slid his finger along her lower lip. "Don't answer now. Take a few days to make arrangements. I'll meet you at the docks on Thursday night after dinner and we'll plan the next step."

He tipped his head and kissed her gently. When she didn't respond, he stilled. He broke away and held her by her shoulders, leveling his gaze. "It's the right thing, Deborah. You'll see." He slid his hands down her arms, taking both hands in his.

She felt dizzy processing his angry greeting ending in a proposal of sorts. She opened her mouth to speak, then shut it. The air hung heavy with what she needed to say, but the moment called for a bit of silence, when the words weren't out there yet. While there were still possibilities.

She took her hands away from his and calmly held them by her side. She met his gaze and spoke softly, even though her heart was beating wildly. "Charlie, I don't think you understand. I want to be with you, but I am always going to live where I can help with Rebecca's children. Always. Until they are grown and don't need me anymore. I promised her."

She watched the information settle, hoping he'd known. Hoping he knew her well enough to know this one thing.

Charlie's expression melted as he processed her words before a stilted smile reappeared. "Aye. You're a devoted auntie. I'm sure you'll want to visit."

Deborah stepped back, but Charlie moved into the space his words had created. "There's more to life than wiping noses and changing nappies, Deborah. Lots more." He slid his hands up her arms gently, resting behind her neck. He pulled her closer, nuzzling her cheek with his lips before tipping his head to meet her lips again. Her resistance melted at his persistence. She met his fire with her own, willing her thoughts to quiet. Willing her heart to be still.

He broke away, a confident smile on his face. He traced her bottom lip with his thumb and winked. "I'll see you on Thursday."

Deborah let him walk away. She watched the place where he disappeared around the corner and listened until the staccato of his shoes on the pavement faded.

CHAPTER 19

The next few days came and went with the usual orderly chaos of their lives. If the children saw Deborah wipe away a tear, kiss Debbie's chubby cheeks more often, or hug them a little longer, they didn't mention it. She caught George watching her more than usual with his perceptive glance, but her quick smile when she met his gaze stifled any questions.

Deborah was clearing the noon meal on Wednesday when Mary Carse knocked once, then peeked her white-capped head through the door. "I'm looking for some biscuit bakers this afternoon. Who wants to join me? The grandchildren at my house are growing weary of their tired old granny."

"You're hardly a tired old granny, Mary, but that would be wonderful," Deborah said, placing the last of the dishes on the shelf and wiping her hands on an apron covering her gray dress. "You are an absolute dearie."

Mary bustled into the room, bringing spice and sunshine in with her. "And I'm taking that sweet babe, too. Just until supper. I'm sure you could use some time to yourself this afternoon."

"I'd love to finish up this week's baking without so much help." She took Jamie down off the stool, trying not to get the dough on his shirt.

"You finish up that bread, then go enjoy the sunshine on this warm November day. That's called taking a break. Do you ken that word, luv?" Mary placed the bottle from the counter into a bag and picked up a squealing Debbie from her cradle.

"I've heard the word before, but I admit it's been a while. You are the dearest." Susannah hung her apron on the hook and inclined her cheek for Mary's kiss.

"Come on Sarah, William, grab Jamie and Susannah. You're coming to Widow Carse's for a bit." The children scurried for their shoes and said goodbye to Deborah on their way out the door.

Twenty minutes later, Deborah grabbed her paisley shawl and started walking. The November wind was chilled, but the sun shone unseasonably warm in a rare Autumn gift. Deborah heard the water before she realized where she'd been heading. Weaving past the bustling docks, she kept walking until the lingering smell of fish dissipated. When she reached the sand, she looked around. The afternoon was quiet, the sun just sinking on the horizon. She made her way down the incline and sat on a rock overlooking the water. It was chilly, but the waves lapping the shore drew her in. She removed her boots and stockings, glancing once more to be sure she was alone. Shoes stowed safely on a rock, she lifted her woolen dress and lace-trimmed petticoat and put her toes in the foam where the sand met the water. Her breath hitched with the cold, but she stayed, feeling the pull of the water as the tide receded.

The water swirled on the shore and she shuddered. She gazed out across the water, undisturbed for a moment by the usual weekday shipping bustle. Her feet sunk further into the sand with each wave, blurring the line between water and shore. Sand sifting between her toes, water pooling around her ankles. Not quite on land. Not quite in water. Neither here nor there, but somewhere between.

There are so few places like this, where you can live in opposites; where you don't have to choose.

Her thoughts swirled like the water, pushing and pulling. Charlie was such a surprise when she thought her courting days were over. She hadn't expected to feel that tug of attraction, that breathlessness. He was rough and temperamental. Maybe even a little selfish. She'd probably tell another woman to be careful. But when they were together, she couldn't think of anything but him. He filled her senses like no one ever had before. She'd have all the fire she could handle if she followed him to Mearns. At 26, it wasn't a stretch to assume that Charlie would be her last chance at a love match. She knew what she'd be signing up for if she showed up at the docks on Thursday.

But when she thought of saying goodbye to Rebecca's children, she felt an almost physical pain. She certainly could come back for the occasional visit, but it would never be the same.

The realization settled that choosing to stay also meant enduring rumors, possibly setting up the children for ridicule or harming George's business. Their unconventional arrangement would be tinder for the gossips' fire. She was strong enough, but at what cost to everyone else?

Deborah swirled her feet in the capricious water one last time and sat on a large rock. She closed her eyes and tried to picture herself with Charlie in Mearns. With Rebecca's family in Dundee. Going back home to Ireland. So often, her path had shifted in ways she didn't understand until later. Now, she knew the next moments of decision were the hinges of a larger door that swung far beyond today.

She opened her eyes and noticed the sun drooping towards evening. It was time to decide.

What is best?

The question lingered for several moments, then Deborah breathed sharply and opened her eyes. The answer that came was the one she hadn't yet let herself consider. It had crept through her thoughts for several days, squirming and wriggling around her consciousness. She folded in on herself as the realization settled, resting her head in her hands as she waited for tears to come. But the well was dry, spent on longer loves.

The creaking of a cart above the bank broke into her awareness and Deborah hurried to stand, brushing the dust off her dress and straightening her hair. She shook out her shoes and stockings and put them back on her feet. She took a few steps, leaving the water behind. The wagon passed, and she realized she could keep walking after all. Several minutes later, she was in Mary's doorway.

She practiced a smile, opening the door a crack. She saw Mary at the table with two of her younger grandchildren, plus Susannah and Sarah. "Is everyone alright for a few more minutes if I get dinner on, Mary?"

"Aye, take your time." She moved a pan of biscuits to the stove. "We need to finish these first, anyway." She put down the pan and made a shooing motion with her hands.

Deborah walked around to the back of the shop and pumped water into a bucket with trembling hands. She fumbled with the back door latch, sending ripples across the water as she walked up the stairs, through the empty kitchen, and into the room she shared with the girls.

She poured the water into the basin on her dressing table and wet a cloth. She drew it across her face first, wiping away the dust, then brought the cloth down her neck. She imagined the water erasing his kisses, his touches. Hoping she could forget what would never be hers. Letting go of so many things. She immersed her hands in the water, enjoying the painful prick of the cold against her skin, then looked at herself in the mirror, studying her face for truth as she dried her hands.

Deborah started some potatoes and cabbage boiling on the stove, set the bread to the heat, and made her way to the bit of filtered light coming through the window. She sat in the worn rocker. Her breathing eventually slowed down, soothed by the back-and-forth motion. She knew she should go fetch the children, but she leaned her head against the chair and closed her eyes instead.

She had been trying to find a way through the puzzle for weeks, searching for somewhere to land between loving the Wright children and keeping Charlie; a road where she could keep the two together, side by side. But now a single path formed. Deborah took a deep breath and let it out again, resolve settling in her mind. When Charlie went to the docks tomorrow, she wouldn't be there.

Rebecca had known.

CHAPTER 20

The light faded through the window as the sunset placed its benediction on Thursday. She couldn't see the docks with the buildings in the way, but she could imagine Charlie pacing there, hands in his pockets, wondering where she was. Deborah closed the curtains. He would know by now.

Deborah sat and ran her fingers along the raised grain in the wood of the kitchen table, tracing it back and forth, focusing on the grooves and valleys, her lips moving in recitation. She jumped when she heard the door open and took a slow breath. *Calm. Neutral.*

George hung up his coat, looked once around the quiet room, and took in her forced expression. "What's wrong, Deb? Where are the children?"

A small smile made its way past her anxiety. He was too perceptive. "All is well. They are all over at Mary's again, getting spoiled with biscuits before dinner. Come sit?"

He quickly crossed the room to her, facing her with a serious expression, the tapped-down weariness clear at close range. He sat in the chair nearest hers. "Out with it. You never sit still. What's wrong?"

She folded her hands, nervously slid them up and down her skirt, then resolutely folded them again. "Please be quiet and just listen?"

He nodded, eyebrows raised.

"It has been brought to my attention that people are talking about the impropriety of my living with a widowed man." George protested, but Deborah held up one hand to stop him. "I will not have the children of Rebecca, the sweetest and purest person made by God, tainted with any kind of scandal. I love all your children more than I've ever loved anything, and I can't leave them. It would break my heart, and I cannot ask them to say goodbye to another mother."

George looked at her with such softness and took her hands in his. They seemed to disappear in his. "I don't care what idle people gossip about, Deborah. You have been an angel to my family. The only way I can work each day is knowing you will care for my children. It's a debt that can't ever be repaid."

She pulled her hands away from his and rubbed them together for a moment. "As I said, I won't have your children teased, and I don't want neighbors giving me looks as I leave this house. I can't stay here like we are now, but I can't leave. The only solution is that..." She paused, then lifted her chin. "Is that you marry me." She continued formally. "I would like to ask you to be my husband." She sat up straighter and looked him directly in the face. "Please."

George opened his mouth, then closed it again. He ran a hand over his late-day whiskers as he tried to find words. They were quiet when they came. "Deborah, I just can't."

She skewered him with her glance. "Did she ask you?"

"Ask me what?" He looked towards the bedroom door, then back to her.

"You know." She held his glance to see the truth, even if he didn't speak it. "Did she tell you to marry me after she was gone?"

He took a deep breath and met her gaze. "She was panicking about the children, about me..."

"Did she ask you?"

George stood. "You've given everything to this family, Deborah. I will never ask you to give the rest of your life away for our sake. We'll make something work, lass. Maybe we could rent you a room from Widow Carse and you could come over in the daytime."

"I promised Rebecca I would care for the children, George! They need me here! Susannah needs me to sing when she wakes up from a bad dream. I need to drag William out of bed in the morning. Sarah is growing into a woman more each day. Not to mention Jamie and Debbie! I won't be their nanny. They need a mother! They need me to live with them as a mother would. I can't leave them, George." Her voice rose as Deborah felt her emotions bubbling out of their careful containment. He was being difficult, and this was as far as she had practiced. She slapped her hand on the table. "So, will you marry me or not?"

He took her by the shoulders. "Look at me, Deb." She bit her lip and met his kind look with fire. "You deserve to have love. True love. Passionate love. You deserve babies of your own and a husband who adores you. I don't know if that's Charlie or someone else, but it's not something I'd ask you to sacrifice. This may seem like a practical option now, but you'll sorely regret it months and years down the road."

He took a ragged breath and stood, his eyes growing moist as he ran both hands through his unruly hair. He turned towards the window. "I have lost my soul twice already. If it weren't for my beautiful children, my feet wouldn't still be walking God's green earth." His voice trailed off and he continued softly, glancing her way. "I've no more love to give a wife, Deb. It's all been given. There's nothing left." He looked at her, begging her to understand. Grief swallowed his eyes as he turned to the window.

She took a long breath and stood to join him, placing a hand on his arm. "George, I don't *want* you to love me that way. I know how much you still love Rebecca. But we're friends, aren't we?" He nodded, looking at the ground.

"Then we stay friends and I get to be your children's mother. I'll take your name, but I keep sharing a room with the girls. I'm perfectly happy there. The only true and pure love I've ever felt is for this family." She willed her voice to stay steady. Willed herself to not care for lesser things.

He was silent.

"George?" She waited until he turned and met her steady gaze. "I just want to stay. Please. It's enough for me."

George looked out the window, his hand coming to rest over hers.

Debating my future...again.

Deborah's foot tapped through the quiet. She decided to go and check the potatoes simmering on the stove when he finally spoke. "It certainly would be best for the children and the easiest solution for me. But are you sure it's the right decision for you? All the way sure?"

"It's the only decision for me. I think I've known for weeks, but it became clear today."

His eyes asked a question that she didn't answer. In the silence, she saw his resolution form. "Well," he said, taking a deep breath and rubbing his hands on his pants, "I can't have my manliness so insulted as to have a wee female propose to me." He winked at her and got down on one knee. He took one of her hands and looked up at her with a little of the normal twinkle back in his eyes.

"Miss Deborah Hasley, as we have been such good friends for the past several years and I know your jokes to be better than average, your cooking to be adequately edible, your temper to be truly Irish, and your heart to be made entirely of gold, I ask in all sincerity if you'll be my wife." His light-hearted manner grew more solemn. "I promise to seek your happiness, as I try to repay the kindness you have shown my family in our darkest hours. I'll not cross the threshold of your bedroom, but in all other ways you'll be my wife."

He paused and smiled a true smile at her, the first she had seen for weeks. "I think this may work out, Deb. It's crazy, but it feels right, doesn't it?"

She nodded, wondering at the emotion gathering in her eyes. She matched his smile.

"So, will you marry me, lass?"

"Aye. I will." Deborah leaned down and patted him on the cheek. She headed towards the stove, where the potatoes were now smoking. She looked at him over her shoulder and tossed a cheeky smile in his direction. "But I asked you first."

CHAPTER 21

ONE YEAR LATER

"Where are you heading?" George put down his planer and brushed the sawdust off his worn apron as Deborah swept downstairs and past his workbench.

"Mrs. Stuart is in labor, and Caroline sent word that she'd need my help with the delivery. She thinks it's twins. That will be two sets, bless her heart." She tightened a gray shawl around the shoulders of her serviceable dark blue dress and headed towards the door. "There's a chicken stewing on the stove and Sarah has the youngest occupied. They've already been fed. If you have a chance, please check in on William. We were working on his number tables for school, but by the time I gathered my bag, he was already drawing an armada on his slate. I should be home before bedtime, God willing."

"So says the unstoppable Deborah Wright." George

chuckled and picked up his planer. "I think I'll just love and educate five children, pluck and roast a chicken for dinner, and scurry off to deliver twins. Ta-ta." He turned back to his work with a shake of his head. "You are amazing, Deb."

"You forgot the part about putting up with an insufferable brother-in-law." She smiled sweetly. "Goodbye."

The bell tinkled behind her as she breezed into the street. The sun was bright for November and the warmth lifted her spirits. She stopped for a moment, willing the warmth to reach places deep inside. George might think that everything was in order, but some days still left her feeling like a spent actress, lines delivered one performance too many. This past year had been the hardest of her life.

The children each dealt with the loss of their mother in their own way. Those first few weeks had seen plenty of tears, tantrums, and silence. But somewhere in the past months, the good days had gently tipped the scale and they seemed to adjust to their new life.

Her marriage to George hardly registered. Two weeks after her unconventional proposal, the children—braided and bowed or slicked and washed—sat in the church along with a few friends and neighbors. Deborah wore a pale lavender dress with a new lace collar and stood with George before the Reverend. Then they all went home for a simmering dinner of Dublin Coddle and she went to bed beside Sarah just as she had done every other night.

But the missing went on and on. Even a year later, a small reminder of Rebecca could leave her fighting back tears. It didn't help that one-year-old Debbie had her mother's glistening blonde curls. As Deborah rocked her little namesake to sleep every night, she twirled ringlets with her finger in that beautiful head of hair, carried away with memories of Rebecca. Making daisy chains in the meadow and crowning her sister Fairy Queen. Helping pin her hair up on her wedding day. Stroking her hair, wet with fever. She was glad then that the rest of the house was asleep. It was safe to cry. There was nowhere else she'd rather be than here, but some days she simply stumbled around in her sister's too-large shoes.

But the sunshine today warmed her a little. *Maybe there is joy still to come.* It seemed hard to believe, but the sun held promises.

Four hours and two babies later, she climbed the stairs to their apartment over the shop, tired but content. Each cry of new life seemed to bring a little more life to her. She opened the door to find everyone on the carpet in front of the fire, William with Debbie on his back, George with Jamie on his, and Sarah with Susannah on hers.

"Well, look at this lovely bunch of horses," Deborah said,

setting her bag down on the table. She pulled a kitchen chair closer to the group and watched their antics. Amazed at their resilience. Grateful that she still had so many people to love.

"We not horses! We cowboys!" Three-year-old Jamie grabbed George's shirt and kicked. After a brief groan, George began to buck and prance, Jamie holding on for dear life and squealing in joy and anticipation of his fate. Eventually, they all ended up on the floor, laughing and exhausted. George fell dramatically on the rug, legs and arms sprawled out.

"Oh! This horsey is tired out," George groaned.

Jamie and Susannah crept up to George's side and poked his ribs, knowing their da's ticklish spot.

He growled and popped up. "It's to jail with you for that!" He grabbed Jamie and Susannah under each arm and dragged them into a pile. He stood and snatched Sarah up like a baby and gently plopped her into the laughing heap. He even snatched baby Debbie and blew a big bubble on her neck before setting her on top of the pile. William scurried out of reach under the table.

George caught Deborah's eye. He raised an eyebrow.

"Oh, no you don't, George!" He was halfway there before she could stand to run. He grabbed her around the waist and hoisted her over his shoulder.

"If you don't put me down right now, I'll scream and the peelers will come to take you away to jail for real, George

Wright!" She whacked his back and squirmed, but he held on tight.

"It seems Aunt Deborah wants to be put down. Shall I put her on top?" He tipped over halfway, grinning.

"Nooo!" they called in unison, scrambling to the four corners of the rug, Sarah pulling Debbie out of the way.

George laughed and gently set Deborah down on her feet.

She hit his arm and tried to keep a stern face, but a smile broke through. He winked at her and growled again, reaching down to grab William's ankle under the table and pulling him across the floor to the rug.

Deborah watched the scene with gratitude, amazed that laughter was heard in the same rooms that had known such pain.

When the house finally fell quiet, Deborah closed the girl's bedroom door behind her with a soft click. She stopped for a moment to take in George's outline against the fire. Her heart hitched a little, watching him there. He was the picture of contentment and industry.

They had settled into the habit of finding their way back to the kitchen after the children were in bed. She usually read poetry aloud while he worked on a carving, but today she'd picked up a copy of the *Dundee Courier* on her way home and was eager for the news.

She settled into the rocking chair, scooting it a little closer to the fire to fight off the January chill. Even dressed in her woolen petticoats, she shivered. George tossed her a blanket from the sofa. She wrapped it around her shoulders and scooted closer to the flame.

"It's chilly tonight, isn't it?" Deborah said.

George didn't look up from the intricate shape taking form in his hands. "That it is. I wouldn't be surprised to see some snow in the morning."

"Mary Carse swears her bones are telling her we'll get at least an inch." Deborah smiled, opening the paper.

George chuckled. "I trust what her bones say. Mary Carse has been an accurate barometer so far." He looked up. "And a good friend. I'm grateful you've had her close by."

"She's a dear. We've been given enough cold shoulders here that a soft, warm one is a welcome change."

She read in silence for a time. Deborah put the paper down and let out a frustrated sigh. George looked up at her huff.

"George, the *Courier* is getting worse and worse. Can I read you part of an editorial?"

"Go ahead. I can tell your ire is up."

"It reads, 'There seems to brood over Ireland a heavy curse, which can neither be expiated by calamities nor mitigated by time. Blessed with soil, she has turned this blessing to bane and produced for the astonishment of Europe, and the multiplication of her own disasters, ragged, slovenly, and starving peasantry. She startles us with the somber records of sanguinary vindictiveness, treacherous cowardice, sullen resentment and degraded superstition, such as darken the annals of no other people.' He goes on and on. How can we be surprised at the coolness of our neighbors when this is what they are told?"

She paused and leaned her head against the smooth wood of the rocking chair. "George, why do people hate the poor?"

His voice was calm, but Deborah noted the vigorous passes of his knife against the wood. "That, dear, is the golden question, isn't it? There's no debate that years of poverty and repression have kept some Irish families from thriving intellectually. We can sit here at night reading poetry, making toys, and chatting about our plans for tomorrow because we've warm clothes and food enough to fill our bellies all day. I wish all those who judge the poor Irish could take a turn working the soil from dawn to dark, eating one meal a day, and sleeping little for the cold. They are judged for their poverty by those who've had the advantage of thinking about more than just staying alive. Who could thrive living like that?"

Deborah was silent for a time, then looked at him. "You're good to the core, George. One of the best."

He looked up, meeting her eyes for a moment longer than

necessary. "Likewise, Deborah. Likewise."

She broke the gaze first and closed her eyes. "Man's inhumanity to man makes countless thousands mourn."

"Burns?" George asked.

"Of course," Deborah answered. She tossed the newspaper to the ground and picked up a book from the small table at her right. "Let's have some more Robbie, shall we? The news is getting me too upset before bed. Would you like me to read aloud? I'm happy to keep the bard to myself if not."

"Always, Deborah. I like to hear you read."

She opened the book and fingered the pink satin bookmark Rebecca used when the book was new. She kissed it and began to read quietly as George worked.

"O my Luve is like a red, red rose
That's newly sprung in June;
My Luve is like the melody
That's sweetly played in tune.
So fair art thou, my bonnie lass,
So deep in luve am I;
And I will luve thee still, my dear,
Till a' the seas gang dry.
Till a' the seas gang dry, my dear,
And the rocks melt wi' the sun;
I will love thee still, my dear,
While the sands o' life shall run."

Deborah paused, a wry grin on her face. "I don't imagine

anyone would describe me as a 'melody sweetly played in tune.' More like a banshee hollering about injustice and ignorance. Not the stuff of poetry, is it?"

George laughed softly. "Oh, I think there's a time to play in tune and a time for a war cry or two. Is that all there is to the poem?"

"No." Deborah paused. She'd stopped on purpose. She glanced at George, then continued. "Here's the rest:

And fare thee weel, my only luve!
And fare thee weel awhile!
And I will come again, my luve,
Though it were ten thousand mile."

They were both silent for a time. Deborah stared at the page, then found the courage to glance towards him. His gaze was on her, a touch of sadness in his eyes.

"It's a charming poem," George said, standing up and brushing a bit of wood dust off his dark brown pants. "But he has it wrong." He paused and took a deep breath waiting for her to meet his eye. "There's no such thing as an 'only luve.'"

He started towards his room before looking back at her. He opened his mouth to say something, then just closed it again. He smiled. "Goodnight, Deb." He held her gaze for a moment, then turned to his room.

Deborah sat, staring at the same page, until the embers died down and the coldness reminded her it was time to sleep.

CHAPTER 22

"William, stop kicking the table leg," George said. "I can't get my kailkenny on my fork." He placed one hand firmly on William's knee as he brought the potatoes and greens to his mouth.

The boy stopped kicking, but Deborah could feel the wooden floor vibrating as he bounced his leg a moment later. George opened his mouth to say something, but Deborah sent him a small head shake. Maybe she shouldn't, but she found William's boundless energy endearing.

George changed the subject. "So, let's have a report from school. What are you learning at the Burgh School, William and Sarah?"

"Nothing," William said.

"Oh, so much!" Sarah replied at the same time.

Deborah smiled. "Sarah, you said the Bailies of the school

were coming to Master Gauld's class for a report. How did that go?"

"We did our recitations, and the younger classes told their arithmetic tables. They said we were very dutiful students." Sarah said with pride.

George smiled at her. "I'm glad to hear it. How about you, William? Did the Bailies come to your class?"

"No. But Rector Murray missed his chair when he sat down today. I had to bury my head in my arms to not laugh. Some boys couldn't help it, and they had to write sentences. I don't think that was fair, because he looked pretty funny on the ground."

Deborah bit back a laugh herself. "That was very respectful of you to not laugh aloud, William."

George turned to Susannah. "And how about you, Susannah? How is Dame school?"

"I passed my letters. And we played Johnny Rover during break time. I was the last tagged, so I won."

"Very good, Susannah. You're a fast runner." Deborah opened her mouth to say something else but was interrupted by a demanding knock at the door. George stood to open it. When Deborah saw Caroline Bethune's granddaughter Fiona standing there, she didn't have to explain anything to the children. They knew what the arrival of the midwife's granddaughter meant.

Deborah took one more large bite of kailkenny and grabbed her bag from the corner and her shawl from the rack. She wrapped it tightly around her shoulders in anticipation of the fall chill and headed out to bring new life into the world.

Thirty minutes later, she entered through the same door, plopping her bag in the corner and dropping her shawl on top of it. George stood from the rocking chair and put Debbie down on the floor. She fussed and he picked her up again to walk towards Deborah. "Well, that was the quickest delivery yet or a false alarm."

"Neither," Deborah replied coolly. "She didn't want me." Deborah reached for Debbie and settled the toddler into her arms, placing an absent-minded kiss on the top of her head.

George looked skeptical. "A laboring woman didn't want a midwife?"

"Not an Irish one. The moment she heard me speak, she informed Caroline that she wouldn't have some slovenly, dirty Irishwoman touching her. She said it would harm the baby to be handled by a howdie with the intellect of her mule."

"She didn't!"

"Those exact words." Deborah sat in the abandoned rocker and pulled Debbie close. "Normally, I give some latitude to women in labor–I've heard language from the primmest little women that would make a field hand blush–but you should've seen the hatred in her face. I believe she'd rather deliver her own baby than have me assist her."

"Oh, Deborah, I'm so sorry." George came and stood

beside her, laying a hand on her shoulder. "What did you do?"

"Nothing. I just picked up my bag and told Caroline goodnight. I wished the spiteful woman a successful birth and walked out the door."

She looked up at him. "George, I was shaking so badly trying not to cry in front of them. But you know what hurts the worst? Caroline said nothing in my defense. I've assisted her for a year and a half now. She knows how qualified I am. But she said nothing. She just looked sad. I count her as a friend, George! I understand I understand she needs the income, but I would've thought she could spare a word in my favor. Her silence wounded me worse than the words."

"Old biddy," George muttered. "I think maybe it's time for you to be out on your own now, anyway. You've certainly had enough experience." He sat down opposite her. "I've been feeling resentment building everywhere. I've not lost business, but I feel weighed and judged each time my brogue peaks out. There's more immigration in this direction, for more than just the harvest season this fall. I think the influx has the Scots on edge."

"Will it get better, do you think?" Deborah asked hopefully.

He shook his head solemnly. "I think it will be worse before it gets any better. It feels like resentment is bubbling just below the surface. I think there's more to come."

CHAPTER 23

That night, the moon peeked through her window. The house had been still for ages, but sleep still evaded Deborah. She replayed the day's conversations in her mind, thinking belatedly of witty and intelligent retorts.

Her body ached with trying to be still, so she quietly slid her legs over the side of the bed. She tiptoed across the wooden floor, the coolness a shock to her quilt-warmed feet. She lit her candle and opened the door, careful not to wake the girls, and quietly made her way to the hearth with its ebbing evening fire. Grabbing the poker, she nudged the flame to life and reached for another log. She stared into the flame and put her hands toward the warmth.

"No wonder you're cold."

The voice startled her, and she turned around to find George sitting on the sofa with a grin on his face. Deborah was suddenly very aware of her thin white nightgown and grabbed a blanket from the rocker. "What on earth are you doing up at this hour?" she asked, wrapping the blanket tightly around her shoulders.

"Probably the same as you. Days like today don't die easily, do they?" He moved over and patted the sofa. "Don't let me stop your midnight plans."

She hesitated a moment, taking in his shadowy shape in the darkness, then stiffly sat down on the far side of the couch. Even though they had spent years in the same household, this was the first time she'd been with him in this state of dress. Or undress. She pulled the blanket closer and smiled weakly.

"So... how are you?" she stammered.

"I'm just fine. And the weather was fine as well. Just fine." George chuckled. "Deborah, I'm not going to bite you. Relax, love. We're past this."

She jutted her chin out. "It just doesn't seem proper. Maybe I'm not used to sitting by a fire in my nightdress with a man."

"Well, that's good to know. But I'm not just any man. I'm your extraordinarily handsome husband." George grinned. "Sitting by a fire with your extraordinarily handsome husband is extremely proper. And could even be a little fun." One side of his mouth turned up in a smile. "But you'd have to come a little closer for that."

"I think I'm just fine over here, thanks." Deborah forced

a wry smile. "And I'm all toasty and warm now, so I'll just head back to bed." She rose, but George gently reached out and held her wrist.

"Stay?" His voice was almost a whisper, with just a little pleading. "I'm sorry to tease you. I don't want you to go. It's so quiet. There are usually children all around us. It's nice to have the night to ourselves."

She hesitated, but felt the same pull into the stillness. Into him. She raised an eyebrow. "No teasing."

"I promise to behave. I'd just like some company. Do you need to talk a bit more about today?"

Deborah sat back down, the tension gone out of her face. "No. But I could use a little peace."

"That I've got. Come here, Deb." He raised his arm, inviting her in. In the daylight, it would have been easy to say that she preferred the rocking chair. Make up some reason to be closer to the fire. But the darkness dissolved her resistance. She simply sighed and slid beside him. He pulled her closer into the crook of his arm. "A little peace and quiet for a good girl who shoulders so much."

Somehow, hearing him call her that put her at ease. Things could continue as they had always been. She told herself that as she nestled further into his arms and lay her head on his shoulder. As she melted into him. As he spread his blanket around her legs and pulled her closer.

The fire was warm and relaxing, and she took a deeper breath than she had all day. She tucked her knees underneath her and settled into the warmth. George hummed into her hair as the darkness gathered around her.

The clock finished chiming two o'clock when George nudged her awake. "You'd better go to bed, Deborah."

She opened her eyes to see his face just inches from hers, his eyes dark and deep. Intense. His breath warm on her face. *Close enough to...*

Deborah sat up abruptly. "I can't believe I fell asleep!"

George smiled and stood up. "Now, who would do that in the middle of the night?" He reached for her hand and squeezed it as he pulled her up. "Thanks for the company, Deb." He held her hand for a moment longer than necessary, rubbing his thumb across her knuckles, looking at her with a mixture of...what? Confusion? Tenderness?

"Now off to bed," he said quietly. Her hand felt cold as soon as he dropped it.

She tossed the blanket back on the rocker and looked back over her shoulder. "Goodnight, George."

He watched her leave, a shadow again in the dying firelight.

Deborah closed the door behind her and snuggled into the blanket's welcome coolness. She lay in bed for a long time before sleep found her again.

CHAPTER 24

A week later, Deborah returned from shopping and made her way up the stairs. The door to George's shop opened, and he stuck his head out. "Can you stop this way first, Deb?"

She paused for a moment then nodded, placing her basket on the landing. Deborah followed him into the workshop. She ran her hand along the edge of a high-backed chair, raw and waiting for stain.

"Is this a new style? I like the tall back."

"Aye. An Englishman came and sketched out just what he wanted. It has nice lines, doesn't it?" George brushed some dust off the seat and gestured towards it. "Try it out."

She sat down, surprised when he pulled up the chair's twin and sat down across from her.

"How would you like an afternoon off tomorrow?"

George asked, his eyes twinkling.

Deborah met his smile. "It sounds delightful. What do you have in mind?"

"I've heard stories about the ruins of an old abbey outside Dundee and I've wanted to take a look. What do you think about going there tomorrow? We won't have many more warm days before winter sets in like it means it."

"Oh! What a great idea. The children would love it, George."

He hesitated, running his hand along the side of the raw chair. "Well, I think they'd like it, but it's a good four miles out of town. I thought you and I could take a long walk and see if it is worth the trek with the children. We may have to hire a cart when we bring everyone."

"Just us?" Deborah's brow furrowed.

"Aye, Deb. Just us. You haven't had a day without children in over a year. I wish I had realized that before. How does a bit of a break sound?"

The break sounded just fine. The company was more concerning. It sounded like…courting.

George smiled and took her hand. "Deborah, you need a change and I wouldn't mind a bit of country air. Sarah will be just fine with the children, and we can ask Mary Carse to look in on them throughout the day to see if they need anything." He squeezed her hand. "Come with me?"

Her head nodded, seemingly without her permission, though she was still confused. "I can pack a lunch."

George grinned and stood. "Perfect. These chairs need a bit more love then I'll be up for dinner soon." He went back to the workbench for his sandpaper as she slowly rose.

She picked up her basket and climbed the stairs, trying to leave the unease behind her. She'd never been alone with George for that long. Ever. And while no one would think twice about her spending the afternoon with her husband, the thought settled with a peculiar combination of lead and butterflies in her stomach.

***

The next morning, she packed a small basket with their lunch. Mary had already come by for Debbie, claiming it was a perfect time for her to get some 'snuggles from a bairn'.

Deborah kissed Sarah on the head and paused, surprised when the fourteen-year-old's crown was near to her chin.

"I think you grew overnight, Sarah. You'll be up to my nose by Hogmanay."

"How tall was my momma, Aunt Deborah? I was only four when she passed so I just remember snatches of her."

"I didn't know Ellen, but I know she was a tiny thing. I think you favor your da, love."

Sarah smiled a little sadly. "I know I look like Da. He says William has my momma's hair, though. I remember her with hair so dark it was almost black."

"From what I've heard, Ellen was as dark as Rebecca was fair, but they had a similar gentle and quiet nature. You certainly have that gentleness, Sarah. I know you've suffered, but always be grateful you had two such wonderful women for mothers. You've been taught well, luv."

Sarah leaned into Deborah's side hug. "Three mothers, Aunt Deborah. I have you, too." She turned and planted a quick kiss on her stepmother's cheek.

Deborah smiled and sighed. "Yes. There's me. I'll never be very sweet and gentle, but I do love you something fierce."

Sarah smiled slyly. "I know that Ellen and Rebecca were quiet and sweet, but I can tell that Da likes you, too."

"Puts up with me, I'd say." She hugged her tighter and planted a kiss on her head. "I'd better go down. You send William to fetch Mrs. Carse if you have any trouble."

"Oh, we'll be just fine. I've puzzles and paints to keep them busy. And I'll just sit on William if he acts up."

Deborah smiled at the image as Sarah moved towards the table where, indeed, she did have a stack of toys and activities ready to go.

"Well then, I'll see you before supper." Deborah grabbed the basket and walked down the stairs. She took a deep breath and opened the shop door. George smiled when he saw her and took off his apron.

"All ready, then? I didn't varnish this morning, so I should be presentable enough." He brushed off a few flecks of ever-present sawdust and joined her at the door, rolling down the sleeves of his white shirt over rippled muscles purchased with constant manual work.

"You look just fine." In truth, he did. Lately, it seemed the tired and haggard look of the last year had been replaced by a bit more life. A bit more spirit lighting up those deep eyes. Deborah realized she was staring and quickly looked away.

He smiled and came near where she stood. "And you, Deb, look lovely."

She willed away the blush that crept up her neck. *Eejit! What will George think?*

Thankfully, he just smiled and took the basket from her arm. Deborah took a deep breath. She didn't know why his compliment stirred her. She didn't want to think about why she wore her second-best dress, a light blue silk with a tucked waist she knew accentuated her curves. She even trimmed her blue coal-scuttle bonnet, adding a yellow ribbon in the back and changing out the flowers. Debbie played with the spent ribbons on the floor while she took the time to form the silly spaniel curls that framed her face and peeked out of the bonnet.

All for a little walk!

They walked in silence for a block or two as Deborah digested her embarrassment over primping for an outing with George. He glanced her way.

"I bet it feels a little odd to be out without the children in tow."

Deborah nodded, glad for his incorrect interpretation of her discomfort. "Aye. I hardly know what to do without trying to keep someone out of mischief." She regretted the words as soon as they fell from her lips, but George simply chuckled.

"If you'd like, I can kick some pebbles dangerously close to glass store windows, or whine for a sugar stick as we pass Jenny Marshall's candy shop so your afternoon feels complete."

She smiled in spite of herself. "Actually, I was hoping that you'd complain incessantly about how tired your feet are and ask me to carry you."

"By the time we get there, it might be you asking for a ride. Are you feeling up to the miles?"

Deborah nodded. "Walking doesn't bother me. And it feels so good to soak up more November sunshine. I admit I'm not looking forward to a hard winter again."

George reached down and took her hand. He squeezed it and his face grew serious. "Deborah, I don't think we'll ever have to live through another winter like the one we passed together. I don't know how we made it through those dark days and back again, but I do know I couldn't have done it without you here with us."

Deborah felt a prick of tears that she shook away. "Nor I, without you. All of you," she quickly added. "Caring for a wee babe allowed little time to sit around and feel sorry for ourselves, did it?"

"No. Debbie's been a blessing all around." He looked at her with such softness that her breath caught a little. "Just like her auntie."

Deborah suddenly became aware that he was still holding her hand. She let go and reached for the basket. "Here, let me take a turn carrying that."

George moved the parcel further away. "I think my arm's better suited to carry it on this long walk, dearie. Besides, you always swing the basket and I'd not like my cream to be butter before we get there."

"There's no cream, and I'm happy to take a turn." Deborah scowled lightly.

"I'll play the gentleman for a bit. Just swing your arms and enjoy the sunshine, love."

They walked through town, then out of it in companionable silence, interrupted by small talk. The dewy gray film of the morning haze faded by the time they arrived at Invergowrie Abbey. They wandered through the mass of fallen walls, all that was left of the ancient abbey. They stopped at a large boulder set prominently behind.

"I've heard there's a legend about the stones. Do you know it?" Deborah asked.

"Well," George began, "Back in 700 AD a priest started building the kirk. The Devil, none too fond of more kirks, was so angry that he started throwing stones from down in Fife. This stone is called the Devil's Stone. There's a few nearer the river called the Goors of Gowrie, and another called the Dark Stane Roundie nearer Menzies Hill."

"Well, I guess that proves the Devil lives in Fife," Deborah said, running her hand along the rough surface.

"And that his aim is off a bit," George added.

Deborah smiled. "The Scottish have their faults, but they do have lovely imaginations. I'd think others may just walk by and call them boulders."

George chuckled and sat down on the dry grass, leaning his back against the rock. He let out a contented sigh. "Ah, I wish we could bottle up this bit of sunshine for January." He closed his eyes against the light and rested his head backward.

Deborah followed suit, the coolness of the rock pleasant against her back after the long walk. She turned to say something to George, but stopped.

How could I have not thought him handsome?

The thought came unbidden. She took in the large arms folded across his firm chest, strong and capable. The long, black eyelashes that were almost a shame to be wasted on a man. The strong jaw and thick, dark hair. She had the foolish notion to reach out a hand and see what it felt like. Would it be coarse and wiry like William's mass of tangled curls, or as silky on her fingers as it looked?

He opened his eyes and turned toward her. His look was casual, but he noticed her startle and turn away. One side of his mouth turned up, obviously aware she'd been staring, but he simply closed his eyes again.

Deborah was properly mortified. She bit the inside of her cheek until she calmed herself and turned to him with a casual tone. "Well, I'm hungry. Should I pull out our lunch?"

George looked over at her, a new awareness in his eyes. She wanted to look away but forced herself to meet his gaze. He casually slid his arm through hers. "Ah, let's stay a moment yet. The sunshine and company are just right."

He paused and glanced at her bonnet. His eyes held a bit of mischief, and he tugged at the yellow ribbon, unsettling the bow. "Soak up a bit of sun, lass."

Deborah swallowed hard and removed the bonnet, placing it at her side. She settled back against the rock, all too aware of the hand that stayed on her arm, snaking past her elbow. All too aware of the empty meadow surrounding them. Surprised by the urge to move into him and lean her head against his strong shoulder again. She tried to breathe normally, but her senses were all jumbled with the warmth of his touch. He traced his fingers almost imperceptibly along her arm and she felt heat radiate through her body.

What would Rebecca think to see us together like this? She squeezed her eyes shut and sucked in a sharp breath against the guilt that crashed against her conscience like a tide held back too long. His voice startled her.

"Maybe it's best to eat that fine lunch you packed after all."

Deborah turned her head and immediately regretted it. His face held tenderness and concern.

She took up the invitation with vigor and stood up abruptly, dusting off her dress. "Indeed." She opened the basket and removed the small blanket she'd nestled on top. Spreading it on the ground, it shocked her to see how small it was when she craved space. Lots of space.

George sat opposite her on the blanket and watched her, his eyes guarded. She silently placed the cut soda bread, cheese, and shortbread on a smooth wooden platter, one that had been a gift from George to Rebecca. It was such a useful size and sat on the table at almost every meal. Deborah didn't think twice about packing it. But now it sat in the middle of the blanket like another guest at lunch. She couldn't pull her gaze from it.

George reached for her hand for prayer, and she reluctantly gave it. They frequently held hands as they gave thanks before every meal, but there was always a pack of children around to fill out the circle. This felt different, intimate.

"Father, for this meal, this day of peace, and the friendship we share, we give thee thanks. Amen."

Deborah opened her eyes and looked intently at George. His smile was sincere and casual. She sighed and smiled back. Friendship. He knew where they stood and wouldn't hold her silly fancies against her. George *was* her friend. Her dearest friend. It didn't hurt anything to notice that a friend was handsome. It need not lead to anything improper. He loved Rebecca, not her.

She felt like she could breathe freely again, unrestrained and unmeasured. It *was* a lovely day, and she wouldn't waste another minute of it with schoolgirl fancies about running fingers through silken hair. She took a drink of lukewarm water from the small flask.

George reached for a large square of shortbread and Deborah slapped his hand. "Just because your children aren't around to see your hedonistic ways, you think you can start with sweets?"

"Absolutely." He snatched the shortbread and winked. "I've been smelling fresh shortbread for four miles now. I have tried the limits of my patience to the fullest."

Deborah shook her head as she reached for a square of cheese. "You're certainly not a very patient person, are you?" She glanced up, cheese midway to her mouth, to see him looking at her intently.

"Maybe not for shortbread, but I am patient, Deb. I'm very, very patient."

The wind blew a strand of hair into her eyes and he reached over to tuck it behind her ear. She realized her cheese still hovered in midair and she lowered it, gulping against the emotion that pricked between them. She forced a casual smile.

"Well, good then." She picked up another piece of cheese

and handed it to him. "You can eat your lunch before you wolf down all the shortbread."

He shook his head and chuckled softly. "Deborah, Deborah," he said, taking the cheese from her and popping it in his mouth.

Their lunch and the walk home were pleasant enough. They talked about the trouble in their congregation since half of the congregation had split from the main body of the state church, about William's propensity to slack in his studies, about making sure Sarah had time enough to associate with the other girls from school.

But George's words were never far from her mind, even as they spoke of lighter things. With each step towards home, her resolution gathered like the dust that clung to her gown.

George might, in a moment of weakness, think there could be something more between them, but she had loved Rebecca longer than him. What were his eight years together with Rebecca compared to the twenty-six she'd shared with her sister?

She might go on picnics with George and enjoy his friendship, but she'd not betray Rebecca. Ever.

CHAPTER 25

The coolness of the December air blew through the door with the children. Their voices jumbled together until Sarah's rose above them.

"Please, Da. Can't we have two pence for Spunk Janet? She's a fortune teller in Cathro's Close off Murrygate, and Molly just had her fortune told. She said that Janet knew everything." She caught her breath. "Please? She really knew everything, just by looking at the lines on Molly's hands. Everything. For just two pence."

George's eyes twinkled as he looked up from his account book at his breathless children crowding the table. "My pence are too precious for a fortune teller." He waited for the disappointed sighs to pass. "But that doesn't mean you can't have your fortune told."

"Oh! Come on, Da," said William. "You know I don't have

that kind of money. Aunt Deborah, please tell him how important this is!"

Deborah came over from the stove and smiled as she sat at the table next to George. "Fortunes do sound fun, but that is pretty expensive for a bunch of blarney."

"Blarney!" Sarah exclaimed. "How could you! Molly isn't a liar."

George chuckled. "Don't get upset, lass. I've got something better for all of you." He went over the hooks by the door and plucked up Deborah's plaid scarf. With a dramatic wave, he placed it over his auburn curls and tied it behind his neck. He pulled the curtains closed and lit a candle from the stove. Moving with exaggerated little shuffling steps, he made his way back to the table and put the candle under his chin. The darkened room bathed in candlelight brought out giggles and whispers. George raised his voice to a whiney, high-pitched sound. "Now, who will be first, dearies?"

Sarah laughed out loud. "You don't know how to read palms, Da!"

"Oh, you smart girl. You are absolutely correct. I don't read palms, but I do read feet. That is an extra training course at fortune-teller school. Who's first?"

"Da!" She shook her head.

"You don't believe me? Well, put those stinky little feet up here on my lap and I'll tell your fortune." He resumed a shrill feminine impersonation. "Come hither, young one, to the Magnificent Moira and we'll see what the future holds for you." He rubbed his hands together as Sarah sat on the opposite chair and propped her feet on her father's lap, a big smile lighting her features.

What a father. Deborah smiled to herself and went to the counter, dipping a rag in the washbasin.

"Here, Moira," she said, "I've heard fortunes can only be told from clean feet."

"It's *Magnificent* Moira, but thank you." George winked at her and washed one layer of grime off of Sarah's feet then lowered his head to inspect her soles.

"Oh! Well, well. I see." He continued his serious study, then traced a wandering line or two, eliciting a giggle.

"That tickles!"

He traced a pattern around her heel. "Aye, I see it all so clearly! This wee line shows you have a secret desire. Secret for everyone but the Great Moira."

"*Magnificent* Moira," Deborah whispered near his ear.

"Whist, unbeliever." He continued to trace circles on Susan's foot. "I see a secret desire to eat as much cake as you want. Oh! And these lines say that you shall enjoy many sunrises. And here, well, this is something!" He stopped, his finger on her pinky toe. "I see true love in your future!"

"You see true love in my toe?" Sarah laughed.

"Shh. Of course, from your little toe. As I was saying, here is the sign of true love in your future. A handsome man will come to marry you and take you away to Italy to live in a villa and eat grapes all day. And you shall have a pet parrot named George." He looked up at Sarah and whispered, "Should I be offended that you named your bird after me?"

She whispered back, "Aye. Very offended. But I do love my fortune. How much do I owe you, Magnificent Moira?"

"Just a kiss, love." His voice dropped a register. Sarah pulled her feet from George's lap, leaned over, and kissed his cheek with a big smack.

"Alright then, who is next?"

Each child took their turn getting their fortune told. William was going on a long voyage and would find true love on the high seas, Susannah would become a famous singer and marry the leader of the orchestra, and James was destined to find a cure for warts, marrying his dedicated nurse. Even Debbie had her fortune told, promising lots of warm milk and true love as a dairymaid.

"Well," George said, taking off his headscarf, "Are you all satisfied with your fortunes?"

They cheered, and George smiled broadly.

"But what about Aunt Deborah?" William asked. "Doesn't she get a fortune?"

Deborah laughed. "I think I'm a little too old for foot-reading. If he had a crystal ball perhaps..."

"Oh, you have to get your fortune, too!" Sarah crossed over to where Deborah sat at the kitchen table and yanked her to her feet. "You have to hear what the Magnificent Moira sees in your future!"

"Very well. If you insist." She let Sarah lead her to the chair opposite George and propped one foot on his lap. Instantly, she felt her face flush. *Silliness. This is George.* She bent down to untie her high boots, but his hands were already there.

He untied the bow and slowly uncrossed the laces. He pulled the boot off and deliberately slid her stocking down to her ankles and paused. She willed him to keep looking at her feet. She was blushing ridiculously.

She laughed in what she hoped was a natural sound. "Well, children, let's see how magnificent your Moira really is."

George then looked up at her, his eyes dark. So full of secrets. Always secrets. But this time, she didn't want to ask what they were. Some were best kept. He held her gaze as he slid her stocking the rest of the way over her heel and off her foot. It dropped to the floor as he held her bare foot in his hand, rubbing his thumbs back and forth over her arch. His hands felt rough and warm on the smooth skin and Deborah's breath hitched. She broke his stare and looked at her feet.

"So, what do you see, Moira?" Her voice cracked, but she managed a smile.

George took a deep breath and exhaled slowly as he lifted her foot slightly. Deborah arranged her skirt as he took her ankle in one hand and began tracing lines with the other. His high-pitched voice seemed a welcome relief to the tension building inside her, and Deborah tried to slow her breathing.

"Oh! This is a fascinating foot indeed! I see a long life ahead for this one. It looks like she has a quick wit and a sharp tongue. Aye, and great intelligence, too." He looked up at her again as he traced a line across her toes.

Deborah jerked her foot back with a squeal. "That tickles, Moira!"

The light sparked in George' eyes. "Oh! We have a ticklish one, do we?" He pulled her foot back, grasping her ankle and tickling in earnest. Deborah shrieked and snatched her foot away, slapping his hand as she stood.

"Well, enough of these shenanigans. It's time to get supper ready," she said.

Susannah frowned and folded her arms across her chest. "But Da, I mean Moira, we all know she is smart. What kind of dumb fortune is that? You dinna promise her true love or anything!"

William shook his head and sighed. "Aunt Deborah is already married to Da, stupid."

The room grew still and George's eyes locked with Deborah. He addressed his children. "Well, maybe you both are right. "Let's finish this fortune, shall we, dearie?" He cocked an eyebrow in a challenge.

Deborah looked at the eager faces of the children surrounding her. She'd rather put her foot directly in the hot stove heating in the corner than back in George's warm hands, but she sat down and met his steady gaze. *Breathe. Breathe.*

"But then right back to work."

He took her foot again in his hands and ran his thumbs up and down the sides, sending shivers through her whole body. He dropped his gaze and took her little toe between two fingers and gave it a wiggle. He looked at his children. "How could I have missed this stubby one!"

He turned his attention to her foot, studying it. "Hum...now I see it. There's an extraordinarily handsome and strong man in your future." He looked back at her until she raised her eyes to meet his. "And as much love as you want. Forever." He squeezed her foot and then set it back on the floor.

The children clapped.

"Much better, Moira!" Susannah said. She turned to Deborah. "Now you have to pay!"

Deborah hoped her gasp wasn't audible. *No big deal. This is George.*

"Well, of course," she said lightly. "Can't be stealing fortunes, now can I? That would be bad luck."

She turned to face him. He looked at her in amusement, one eyebrow cocked. He took her hand and said in a low voice, "Technically, you received two fortunes, lass. Just a reminder."

She swallowed and planted a quick peck on his right cheek, her hand still in his. His cheek felt rough with the day's stubble and warmer than she expected. She trembled a little as she pulled away. "There's one," George said quietly into her ear, sending shivers down her spine.

"You are a scoundrel," she whispered back, pulling back to kiss his left cheek. Deborah caught his eye before she pulled away and wished that she hadn't. She put on a merry face, and walked towards the stove, willing her heart to slow. Her body to relax. And her heart to behave.

CHAPTER 26

"It's so quiet." George gently closed the door behind him.

Deborah started. She hadn't heard him come up the stairs from the shop below. She put a lid on the pan on the stove and moved it off the direct heat.

"I was singing to Debbie to get her down for her nap, and Jamie fell asleep on my bed, lying right on top of his wooden train. He's quite out."

She whisked around and ran straight into his chest, her face colliding with solid muscle. George chuckled and put both hands on her upper arms, pulling her back a few inches. "Slow down, lass! I was just going to take a peek at what miracle you've been working on the stove."

"Oh, it's just potatoes with a bit of mutton and spice." She looked straight ahead, afraid to raise her head to his. Afraid he'd know their proximity ruffled her beyond belief. Yesterday's fortune-telling fiasco had her brain all muddled again.

He gave her arms a quick squeeze and let go. "I smelled your creation all the way downstairs. You make a man hungry for his dinner even when it's hours away."

She took a calming breath and put a few more steps between them. "I'm glad you like my cooking, George."

George bridged the distance again, taking a small step forward. "You make it sound like you're a newly hired girl, Deb." She gave a noncommittal shrug. He looked at her until she met his eyes, his brow wrinkling at the tension he sensed from her. "There's so much I like about you. The fact that you keep us all fed is just a little bonus."

Deborah shook her head. "You don't need to flatter me, George."

His eyes darkened and he took another step closer. "Deb," he began.

She moved past him towards the stove, pulling off the lid and stirring the pot she had just stirred. He moved with her, turning her to face him when she put the spoon across the lid. He lowered his gaze and ran his hands up and down the length of her arms.

"Deborah, you can run away to the stove as often as you like, but I'll not leave the conversation until I'm sure you understand that I don't think of you as my cook." She met his eyes, deep and dark with emotion. She swallowed hard as he brought one hand to rest on her cheek. "I don't think of you as just my children's nanny or our housekeeper." His forehead moved to touch hers.

The space crackled with emotion as their breath mingled in between. She could see the rise and fall of his chest, could almost hear his heartbeat in rhythm with the pounding in hers. Deborah felt her resolve weaken. It would be so easy to take one more step forward and disappear into his arms. Into that wonderful smell of wood and warmth. Into his love. She found herself leaning into him almost against her will. She needed more. She needed him. Her hands came up to his chest and his breath caught.

He brought his hand behind her neck, running his thumb along her jawline as his other arm came behind her, bringing her in the last few inches. He nuzzled his nose into her hair as his hand splayed across her back. "And sweet Deborah," he whispered in her ear, "I certainly don't think of you as my sister."

His words were like a winter breeze through the window, invading the warmth building inside. She was already moving away as his lips touched hers.

"But I am." Her voice was laden with emotion and only a whisper came out. She moved her hands to hang obediently at her side. "That's what I am. Your sister-in-law."

His chest rose and fell in deep breaths and he pinned her with a look that took her breath away. All the secrets were gone from his eyes, and he didn't try to hide the longing.

"Deb, you are my wife." He paused, grasping her hand. "And I'm in love with you." He gently tugged her to him.

She came one step closer on instinct, then groaned and ripped her hand away. She stumbled to the table and sat down on a chair, putting her head in her hands, squeezing her eyes against the flood of emotion.

She sensed George behind her before she felt his hands on her shoulders. His voice was low and comforting. Like warm honey. "Deborah, we have all the time in the world. I'm sorry if I overstepped where we are. I thought…" His voice trailed off.

He rubbed her shoulders and kissed the top of her head. The silence stretched out between them. When he spoke again, the rugged edge had left his voice. "So, I saw the Castle Theatre has a touring company coming through on Saturday evening. It's a soprano singing traditional Gaelic songs. I thought you might like that? Would you like to go?" His voice was tentative, measuring her.

"No. Thank you, but I don't care to go to a concert with you." She knew she sounded petulant, but she didn't care. She felt tears threatening behind her eyelids and she wanted this conversation over. Now. She stood and faced him.

He flinched at her tone, but resignation stole over his features. He continued quietly. "I'm sorry if I didn't think that through. Maybe it's best to go somewhere where there aren't any memories of you and Charlie together."

She was confused for a moment then ran a hand over her

face in frustration. "You think I don't want to go to Castle Theatre because it's where *Charlie* and I went together? Because there are too many happy memories of a past love?" She was getting heated now, the extremes of emotion bringing on an avalanche she was powerless to stop.

He nodded hesitatingly. Sensing her anger. Searching her face for clues.

"I assure you, George, I haven't given Charlie a second thought for over a year. You were right about him all along, you know." She swallowed and stared him down. "But since we're talking about memories, maybe you'd care to explain to me why you are trying to court *me*, under the very roof where you shared a perfect life with my sister. What about betraying those precious memories? What about betraying her love?" Deborah hugged her arms around her middle, trying to hold the pain inside.

"George," her voice dropped to a whisper as she looked away. "How could we?"

George looked as if he'd been slapped. Deborah knew she'd opened a door that should have remained closed. Their friendship lived on a fragile precipice of unspoken things. But the door was open now so she finished walking through. She choked back the emotion that clogged her throat and looked up into his eyes.

"I will take care of all of you for the rest of my life. It was the only thing Rebecca ever asked of me, and I promised her that I would. I'll be your friend. I'll cook for you and keep your house. I'll love your children with my whole heart. But I will not betray her, George. I just can't."

George opened his mouth to say something, then closed it again. He simply nodded, pain and resignation filling his eyes. Tears won out over her will, and she covered a sob with her hand. She ran into her room and shut the door, leaning against it for support. A moment later, she heard the door to the stairwell shut and the sounds of a muffled hammer fill the air.

Her tears were of the missing kind, as always, but now they were tinged with a new kind of loss. She knew her words had put an abrupt end to George's courtship and would tighten the reins that had slacked these past weeks. *It had to be done. Now, we can get back to normal.*

She was all dried up by the time the stairwell door opened again. Debbie awoke from her nap with the commotion of the children coming in from school, full of laughs and squeals. The toddler let out a yell and kicked the foot of her small crib. Deborah smiled, nuzzling into her softness as she picked her up.

"We'll have to get Da to make you a new bed soon, won't we, big girl? You are just about out of that one."

"Mamma!" Debbie slapped both her hands on Deborah's cheeks.

Deborah kissed Debbie as she turned towards the mirror. The sight almost took her breath away. The child looked so perfect, but the mother was all wrong. Rebecca and Debbie had made such a striking pair, sharing the same golden curls and rich brown eyes. It almost looked like Rebecca held a miniature version of herself. Deborah's own dark, straight hair, pulled back into a proper knot at her neck, stood out in sharp contrast to the baby's wild blonde curls.

Rebecca, your baby may think I'm her mother, but I'll not let your husband think I'm his wife. We won't forget you.

Debbie squirmed until Deborah placed her on the floor. She toddled off in search of the happy commotion coming from the other room. Deborah glanced at Jamie's sleeping form, still out for the count. She opened the door for Debbie and was met with hugs from all levels and overlapping stories of the day's adventures. A measure of peace filled her heart.

Purpose. Work. Service. Family. That was all she needed. That would be enough.

Over the next couple of weeks, they fell into a new pattern. She stood by George's side as they cleaned the dishes, careful not to bump his shoulder. She sat on the floor as they played with the children. Listened quietly as he read from the Bible in the evening. He talked about his furniture and she talked about the babies she brought into the world. He was kind and considerate, watching the children and taking over the chores when she was gone with a prolonged delivery. He thanked her for dinner. He thanked her for mending his socks. He told her she looked lovely each Sunday morning and held out his arm as they walked smiling to church. He said goodnight every evening as she went to her room early with the children. The politeness was stifling.

Deborah kept tight control of her eyes, of her body. She looked away when she caught him looking at her. Moved away when he stood too close.

Dinner was the hardest. She focused on the children, but George's presence opposite her was too large to ignore. His hair was wilder than usual. It flopped across his brow every time he bent to eat. He had unbuttoned the top two buttons of his shirt against the heat from the glowing fire and that small space between his neck and chest begged for her notice. She focused instead on the food on her plate and pushed the stewed cabbage and potatoes around a little longer. She noticed Sarah doing the same. William piled his potatoes up in a stack and waited for them to fall, his chin on the table. Susannah, Jamie, and Debbie all ate in silence.

There's no reason my dour mood should affect everyone else.

Deborah forced a brightness to her voice that she didn't feel and pasted a smile on her face. "Who would like to go to the Greenmarket with me tomorrow? Perhaps we can make a stop by Robbie Salmond's booth for some gingerbread or find another treat?"

Susannah and Jamie readily agreed, and even Debbie clapped her hands in oblivious agreement.

Sarah brightened. "I hope that Professor Cottrill is there again!" She turned to her father. "You should have seen it last time we went. He ate up three pounds in coins while he was under the water in a tank. He came out and spit it out right in front of us!"

William shrugged. "That's nothing. I like Wombwell's Menagerie the best. Giraffes, gorillas, and kangaroos are better than an old man trying not to drown and choke at the same time."

Sarah huffed. "But that only comes once a year at fair time."

The children kept talking back and forth about adventures at the Greenmarket. Deborah struggled to nod at their enthusiasm about Dundee's famous sugar herts and curlie murlies, putting what she hoped was a pleasant expression on her face.

Would they never be done eating? Tonight's dinner seemed to last longer than usual, and she couldn't wait to retreat behind a book in her room after evening chores. She forced one more bite of bread down, then stood to take her plate to the basin.

She felt George's gaze boring into her back. He took a deep breath, then turned to his left, where William's potatoes toppled onto the table. "Sarah, William, see to the dishes. Aunt Deb and I are going to take a little stroll. Susannah and Jamie, can you watch Debbie sharp as a hawk? She'll try to follow us."

He waited for his children's acknowledgment, then stood. He walked to the basin and held out a hand for Deborah, patient insistence on his face.

"I don't care to take a walk, George," Deborah snipped.

He didn't move but raised his eyebrows until she took his outstretched hand. She took it, her lips pressed together in a thin line.

George looked back at the children who watched from the table. "We won't be gone but a minute." Deborah set her plate down with a clatter but took the shawl he held out to her and allowed him to lead her toward the door. Debbie started to cry at their departure, but Susannah rose from her chair and was already playing peek-a-boo as the door closed behind them.

Deborah jerked her hand back as soon as the door was closed and faced George on the landing. Her voice was clipped. "I don't need you to take me for a walk like I'm a mopey child or snappy dog, George."

He shook his head and snatched her hand again, guiding her down the stairs. "We're having this out, Deborah. And aye, you look very much like a snappy puppy right now. Out you come for your walk."

When they exited onto the quiet street, he turned to face

her. "Walk or sit?" He motioned to the brick window sill behind her. She plopped down, staring straight ahead. He sat quietly beside her.

He reached for her hand, but she snatched it away, turning her head to watch a calico cat slink behind the corner.

"Deborah, look at me." His voice was kind but offered no option to disagree.

She looked at him. *Nonchalant. Relaxed. Unaffected. Unconvincing.*

He read her with a sad smile. He tipped his head empathetically and opened his arms wide. "Come here, you miserable little thing."

She wanted to stay where she was, to not need him, but after a moment's hesitation, she went to him just the same. Her throat squeezed tight against the threatening tears as he pulled her closer, resting his chin against her head. She struggled to hold back betraying tears that seeped out under her eyelids.

"Breathe, luv." His whisper against her hair sent shivers down her spine, but she obediently took a deep breath.

George chuckled. "That's better. You're like a little thundercloud you know. The clouds gather so dark and stormy when you're troubled. The only path to clear skies is to let the rains come. Go ahead and cry, Deborah. You've never been good at holding it all inside. It's not in your nature."

Though she tried to keep them in, even talking about crying brought the tears. He just held her close. After a few minutes, she regained her composure and pulled away, wiping her nose on her handkerchief.

George took her hand again, and she didn't pull away this time. He gave her a small smile. "Now, what's the problem? My emotional, fiery, opinionated Deborah has gone away, and there's this quiet, stoic, unhappy woman left in her place. I know I'm responsible for upsetting you, but we need to find a way back. I'll not have you pained at my hand. I'll not lose your friendship."

"But how can we go back to being friends? I think we've broken everything we had, George."

"I'm sorry that I've upset you, but I'm nothing but grateful that you're in my life, however you want to be in my life." He lifted her chin so she was forced to meet his eyes. "Deb, I love you." He looked at the ground. "I can't expect you to feel the same, but I'm hoping that in time you might. I know I'm older than you and not what you had in mind for a husband, but I do truly love you. You need to know that. It's like I told you years ago, I don't know how it's possible for a heart to care again, but it is. It seems like all the love that's there gets to stay, and new places are created for new loves. Loves that are just as true as the ones that came before."

He dropped her hand and ran his hands through his hair, leaving it messy. He turned to look at her. "But the most important thing to me right now is that you are happy. You will always be my friend. You just get to choose whether you want to be my sister...or my wife."

He turned his head to watch the same cat slink past them on the street, letting his words and the silence settle.

Her voice, when it came, was a whisper. "I don't know."

His voice was low and steady. "That's fine. Just let it be for now." He bumped her shoulder with his. "And just be at ease, will you? It's painful to watch you try to pretend I don't exist."

Deborah smiled, despite the tears that made a slow trickle down her cheeks.

"Besides, how could such a glorious specimen of manhood fail to escape your notice? It's asking too much of anyone, really." George puffed out his chest, flexing his muscles. He wagged his eyebrows at her.

She bumped his shoulder in return. "I suppose if there was such a man around, it would be difficult indeed."

She met his eye shyly, glad to see a grin on his face. She wiped a hand across her damp cheeks and took a deep breath.

He took her hand again and pulled her up next to him. He wrapped his arms around her and gave her a big squeeze, lifting her off her feet. "Let's go back inside, you complicated little mess. We've a family to love."

CHAPTER 27

Deborah knocked on Mary Carse's door the next morning, a loaf of soda bread in her hand.

Her neighbor's cheery voice sounded through the wood. "Well, come in dear! There's no use standing outside when you're holding something tasty for me."

Deborah smiled and walked through the rough door opening, ducking a little at the small entrance. Deborah smiled at the domestic picture that greeted her. Her neighbor sat knitting by the fire in a black linen dress, crisp white collar, and carefully coiffed gray hair. A small lace cap perched on her head like frosting on a cupcake. She looked up with a smile that moved all the leathery wrinkles around on her face in ways Deborah thought beautiful.

"How did you know I had something tasty for you?" Deborah asked.

"I smelled your baking all morning. Since you're the only one who comes to see me this time of day, I put the two together. Aren't I smart as a whip?" Her eyes twinkled as she set aside her knitting.

"You certainly are, Mary." Deborah set the bread on the worn table. It wobbled when she bumped it with her hip as she passed into the sitting area. "You should have George tighten up your table, Mary. The legs are loose."

"Oh, it must be from me kneading my bread in angry protestation about my pension. How I wish we still had Reverend McNeil at St. Andrews. Reverend Ewing has cut me down to four shillings. How's a body supposed to live on that, I'd like to know?"

She lowered her voice to a whisper. "Don't tell a soul, but when I'm kneading me bread, I pretend that it's his face I'm pounding on. How do you like that? And me husband a deacon in his own day." She laughed out loud.

"You, dear, are very terrible. I am sorry about your pension, though. I know things are already tight. Reverend Ewing is a hard man who seems to have missed all the scripture about caring for the widow and fatherless." Deborah paused and proceeded carefully. "Mary, have you thought of joining the dissenters? You know about half of the congregation has left. I can't tell you what a different feeling there is now. Even just knowing we have a say in choosing our pastor with no more aristocratic appointments feels like a breath of fresh air."

"Oh, I know that reform is needed, but I'll stay just the same. That old church is where I was wed and where my babies were baptized. It will be where I rest my bones next to my husband when my time comes. I'm too old for change, but I am glad that it is coming. It's long overdue. Especially when the clergy holds back my pension."

"I understand. But you know you won't go hungry as long as we're neighbors."

"I ken, luv." Mary patted Deborah's cheek as she drew a chair up beside her. "Now, what did you bring me?"

"Just some good Irish soda bread from a good Irish neighbor," Deborah said with a wink. "There's nothing like good soda bread with jam. Though I will stoop now and then to put some of Keillers good Dundee marmalade on it in a pinch."

Mary laughed. "If only you could learn to express your opinions, love."

"If only you could!" Deborah retorted.

"I dinna ken how George handles you, dearie. I'm sure he's got his hands full." Mary laughed, then stopped as she registered the deep blush that overtook Deborah's face. "Well, now, that's interesting," she smiled slyly. "Is it the thought of George handling you that's got you all pink in the cheeks?"

Deborah swatted at her. "Oh, stop it, Mary! You know very well that George and I have an… arrangement. It's not like that." Deborah placed a hand on her hot cheek, well aware that she was completely flushed beyond any hope of hiding it.

Mary considered her, wrinkles bunched up in the corners of her eyes. "Well, considering this is the first time I've seen you blush like a schoolgirl, I'd say that this 'arrangement' might be changing a little."

"No." Deborah sat in the wooden chair next to the table. It tottered under the force. "Nothing is changing about our arrangement, Mary. You know how Rebecca loved George with her whole soul. I would never betray my sister. I'm simply watching out for her family in her honor. I promised her I would, and that's what I'm doing."

She couldn't stop the quiver from her voice or the hot tears that hung on her lashes. She put her elbows on the table and lowered her face into her hands. Her voice was tight and quiet. "I could never betray her. It would break my heart."

Mary leaned in closer and rubbed slow circles on Deborah's back. "Maybe there's even a little more to it than that? Let's get it all out."

Deborah raised her head to look at Mary. Her face crumbled as indecision melted with a gush of words. "I didn't mean to! I don't even know how it happened! I hate myself but I can't help it. Oh Mary," she looked up at her friend, "I'm in love with Rebecca's husband." She buried her head in her arms on the table as sobs shook her body.

"Sweet one," Mary said consolingly, "I think what you meant to say is that you are in love with *your* husband."

"But he's not mine."

"Do you have a marriage certificate? Did you say 'I Do' before God and man?"

Deborah looked up and reached into her pocket for a handkerchief, pulling it out to wipe her face. She shook her head in frustration. "You were there, Mary. But you know I didn't really mean it."

"Aye, I was there. And along with everyone else who was there, I ken you were marrying so soon after Rebecca's death not out of passion, but out of practicality. I ken hateful rumors were taking a stroll around the block. I ken you were sacrificing yourself and your future chances to honor your sister's memory and care for that house of children. I wished you all comfort after so much tragedy. But you ken what else? I would bet my biscuits that every person there had one other wish, as well. We wished that there might be enough healing balm in your souls and grace in this sad world that eventually you might find true joy and love together. I ken that has been my wish all along."

Deborah raised her head, surprise momentarily stopping the tears.

"And now, it does my heart good," Mary wiped the back of her hand across her own eyes, "to hear you say that you have found that love." Mary placed a hand on Deborah's cheek. "Child, you deserve to be loved."

Deborah looked at Mary with a mixture of hope and despair. Her voice was a whisper. "But what about Rebecca?"

Mary smiled. "Do you truly think that Rebecca intended that the two of you should be lonely together for the rest of your lives? That you would never get the chance to be cherished as a wife or have your own child?" She clucked and shook her head. "Rebecca was kind and sweet, but she wasn't stupid, dear. What did she think would happen, leaving you in the house with that good-looking man? I think she planned this out. All of it."

Deborah was silent. She blew her nose, then clasped the handkerchief between her hands on the table. "You don't think she would hate me? She wouldn't be devastated that I love George, too?"

Mary shook her head and put a hand over Deborah's. "I think she'd be delighted that her plan went so well."

Deborah considered her friend's words in silence for a while. "But what do I do? I'm not sure I can ever get over the feeling of betrayal I get every time I get close to him. I feel so guilty. I'm not sure what comes next."

"Time, luv. Just give it time. I'm sure you'll both figure it out." Mary winked at her.

Deborah ducked her head and smiled. She took a deep breath and stood. "Well, I have plenty to think about." She stood and patted her hair back in place and tucked the well-used handkerchief back into her dress pocket. "Enjoy your soda bread, Mary. I've got a houseful of children and a good-looking husband to get back to." She took Mary's hands and kissed her cheek. "Thank you. Truly."

"You're welcome, lass. Thanks for the bread—and for letting an old widow have a little excitement now and again."

Deborah closed the door behind her. She turned towards home, but stood on the busy street for a moment, letting Mary's words settle in her heart.

CHAPTER 28

Deborah was quiet during dinner. She felt a shyness towards George that she had a hard time hiding. Goodness, she blushed when he looked at her and asked to pass the Cullen skink. The fish soup trembled as she scooted it across the table. He raised an eyebrow at that.

Deborah concentrated on the children and dinner. When they were done eating, she asked George if he could help William finish up his schoolwork, eager to clean the dishes in silence. She wasn't ready to be alone with him again until she had sorted through the workings of her heart.

She gave Debbie a pot to bang on while she finished the dishes, and hazarded a glance towards the table. Sarah had just finished wiping it down while Susanna straightened the chairs. Jamie sat on the floor and dumped out his blocks with a crash. George bent down and scooped up a few. He turned toward William and arranged the squares to explain an arithmetic problem. He must have sensed her gaze because he turned towards her, smiling a slow smile at catching her stare. He gave her a wink and sent his attention back to the blocks in front of his son.

Her heart puddled. She grasped the edges of the stove and leaned forward, sending a silent prayer heavenward. *Is this right, Lord? Can I love him?*

She closed her eyes and tried to feel the answer in the commotion, but only heard the clatter of blocks and the chatter of children. She sighed and finished cleaning up, then scooped up Debbie. She bounced her in her arms into the bedroom to change her into a nightdress. All ready for bed, they headed towards the rocking chair. Deborah bent down to snatch a few books and sat with the toddler on her lap.

"Alright, luv. Which one tonight?"

Debbie reached for her favorite fairy stories.

"This one?" Deborah asked.

Debbie nodded and snuggled closer, her little body melding with her own. Deborah began reading the story of a changeling princess as George finished up with William. She heard the arithmetic book snap shut and George's chair push away from the table. He headed for the door.

"I'll be back in a bit. I need to add another coat of varnish to Miller's bed frame."

Deborah nodded without meeting his eye and kept reading. By the time she started the second tale, all the children were gathered around her on the floor. They'd never come when invited, but she loved how the enchanting stories drew them in regardless. Soon, Debbie's head felt heavy against her chest and Jamie leaned lazily against Sarah's shoulder. Deborah smiled.

"That's enough for tonight. To bed, luvs. It's late." She whispered.

William groaned, but stood with the others. She kissed Sarah, Susannah, and Jamie and rumpled William's hair. He took Jamie by the hand and went down the stairs to their corner of the workshop. Sarah and Susannah made their way to the bedroom. She snuggled Debbie closer for a moment, comforted by her slow and even breath. She stood and headed towards the bedroom, closing the door with her foot and shushing the giggling girls, already tucked into their beds. A moment later, with Debbie all snuggled under the covers, Deborah made her way back to the main room.

George was still downstairs in his shop, so she added a log to the fire and settled into the chair with the day's newspaper, trying to still her breathing. Her heart skipped a beat every time she heard a sound from downstairs, aware of all his movements. Aware he'd walk through the door at any time. Aware she wanted him to.

She tried to focus on the newspaper and was momentarily distracted by a story about boxing, of all things. She became so intent on the article that she gasped when the door opened and George walked through.

He chuckled at her surprise. "Who did you expect, Deb?"

She was instantly flustered but tried to calm herself. "The boys are settled?"

"Jamie was already snoring and William was reading by lantern when I left. It was a ghost story, so don't be surprised if he's upstairs before long, pretending not to be scared."

"He's got a love for adventure stories for certain." She paused and returned to the paper, eager to keep the conversation on safe topics. "Did you read about the boxing tragedy, George?"

"I've not seen the *Courier* today, but I know the match was set to take place last weekend in Salcey Green. An Irishman and a Scot, no?"

"Aye. Sandy McKay was billed as the 'Champion of Scotland' and Simon Byrne is known as 'The Emerald Gem.' Byrne won but left McKay beaten beyond recognition. He died from his injuries the next day. Byrne was charged with manslaughter, but was almost instantly acquitted."

She put down the paper with a sigh. "How tragic! Forty-seven rounds of two bare-fisted men trying to cause harm to each other. What would lead someone to take part in such a thing?"

George let out a puff of air. "A tragedy, no doubt. But the prize was two hundred pounds. Most poor men would take a beating for that purse." He shook his head. "I'm just worried about the reaction of our neighbors. This fight was more about pride than boxing. The Scots were talking up

McKay for weeks. We'll not be the most popular folks on the block for a time."

"For a change," Deborah mused wryly. A sharp knock interrupted their conversation. George rose instantly and found their friend Nathan McDonald bending over, breathless.

"On with your coat, man. There's a riot tonight, and it's not looking pretty to be Irish right now."

"What's happened, Nathan?" George asked, Deborah instantly at his side. She grabbed his arm as Nathan caught his breath.

"An Irish bloke named Thurrel was wagging his tongue at a pub tonight, bragging on about Byrne. Then some Scottish bloke named Heron argued that the fight wasn't fair and Thurrel started throwing punches. Heron fell, but Thurrel kept kicking him on the ground. Heron's folks was so mad they set on Thurrel and all the other Irish at the pub with bottles and rocks. It just exploded from there. Any Irishman in the streets is getting the lights knocked out of him, and they've demolished the Catholic chapel at Meadowside. I stepped out when I heard the commotion and saw William Coyle just down the other end of Bucklemaker being dragged from his shop by that baker named Robertson and John Adamson, the weaver one shop down. I didn't wait to see what happened but started running. I tell you, no Irishman's safe in the city tonight. I'm getting out of here and heading to the Hill Balgay to wait until things settle down. There's more heading that way. You coming?"

George shook his head and put his hand over where Deborah's rested on his arm. "I'll not leave my family, Nathan. We'll take our chances here."

"Not a woman's been hurt tonight, George, but there's not an Irish storefront from here to Hilltown that's not been harmed. And not an Irishman, either. Unless you want your family to watch your beating, you'd best head out with me now."

George looked down at Deborah. She bit back her worry and looked at him steadily. "Sounds safer without you here, George. We'll be fine. I'll bring the boys up from downstairs and we'll hunker down in the bedroom." She turned to the window at the sound of shouting. "Just go. I can hear noise coming from down the street."

He gave her a long look, then nodded. He grabbed her hand and kissed her palm, his eyes never leaving her face. "I'll be back soon. You've got the boys?"

"Aye. Now just go. Please be safe." She felt the tears welling up but stuck out her chin. She released his hand and gave him a gentle push towards the door when he paused. "Run, George."

They were gone in another heartbeat, and Deborah hurried down the stairs after them.

"William, grab your blankets and your lantern. Light the way upstairs for me. You're sleeping in my room tonight."

William groaned. "I'm not sleeping with the girls, Aunt Deborah!"

Her voice rose. "You're for upstairs tonight, lad. I don't have time to explain. Just get your blanket and light the way right this minute."

William didn't brook an argument but gathered the bedding as Deborah lifted Jamie into her arms. "Light our way, William."

He shone the lantern up the stairs and safely into the bedroom. As soon as Deborah deposited Jamie beside the sleeping Susannah, she heard a cacophony of angry voices from the street just outside the window. Her heart sank as the sound of their front store window shattering filled the night air.

William's eyes went wide. Deborah turned to him.

"William, let's try to keep everyone asleep. You are not to open this door for any reason. You are not to come out. If you hear anything, pretend to be asleep. Do you understand?"

He nodded, fear in his eyes. She kissed him soundly on the forehead. "It will all be alright. Some men are throwing a grand tantrum around town tonight, but it will be over soon. Your da has run to safety and we'll be safe here. You'll stay put?"

He nodded again and Deborah walked briskly for the door and closed it behind her. She stopped at the hearth to stoke the fire to a roar, hoping the light could somehow ward off the darkness that gathered around their home. She put the poker back on the hook by the hearth, then took it down again, fingers trembling. *It would have to do.*

She pressed her ear to the door, grateful for the silence from downstairs. Apparently, the mob moved on without looting the place. She slumped down and leaned against the door, listening as the night air filled with the din of anger and hatred, the silent animosity of her neighbors gurgling up from its hibernation. She closed her eyes, nestled the poker at her side, and said her second prayer of the night. *Keep him safe, Father. Keep them all safe.*

She must have dozed for a time because the loud banging from the other side of the door startled her awake. She glanced at the clock, barely visible with the dying fire, and saw it was just past four in the morning. Steeling herself, she opened the heavy door with a deep breath.

Two men wearing the rough-woven colorless attire of the working class pushed past her, bringing the smell of alcohol and unwashed body in their wake. Their eyes were almost feral as they turned in her direction, the anger ripe in their voices. "Where's your paddy, missus?"

"He's visiting friends. He's not here." *Direct. Firm. Unafraid.*

The tallest of the two brushed past her towards George's door, while the heavyset man headed towards where the children were sleeping. "Well, we'll just take a look, won't we?"

She hurried to the door before him, her heart beating a march in her chest. "You can look within, but you'll not take a step inside. There's naught but children sleeping within and you'll startle them. Your business is with my husband, and not with them. I give you my word he's gone."

The heavyset man came back from his search of George's empty room. He laughed as he shoved her aside with a leathery hand. "Well, that's pretty now. Why, the word of the Irish is truer than true, aren't it, Alan?"

"Good as the gold at the end of the rainbow, I'd say." He laughed at his joke, spewing foul breath in her face. He followed the other man into the room. One opened the standing wardrobe and the other looked under the bed. They peered at the sleeping faces one by one. Deborah bit her cheek, desiring with her whole soul to force them from the room, or at least give them a solid tongue-lashing. Instead, she remained at the door, fingering the fire poker that was hidden in the folds of her brown silk skirt and willing her breath to calm.

Finally, they turned in unison towards the door and strode past Deborah without a glance. The one she'd heard called Alan tossed a final comment over his shoulder as they left.

"No mistake about it, we'll be watching for your paddy to come back home. All the Irish will know just how much we appreciate you stealing our jobs and souring our country with your papist claptrap. God-fearing Protestants won't put up with it a day more."

They slammed the door, shaking the frame, and trampled down the stairs. She cringed as she heard wood splinter and metal tools clang to the floor. Then, silence.

Deborah dropped the poker and rushed into the bedroom. William's head shot up and she hurried to his side, kneeling by his makeshift bed on the floor.

She took him in her arms. "It's all over, luv. Were you awake?"

"I've been awake all night, Aunt Deborah. I wanted to come out, but I kept my promise. I was a good faker, wasn't I? They thought I was asleep as can be."

She stroked his hair. "You were a very good faker, William. I'm just sorry you had to hear those mean words. I do believe we're safe for the night. Do you think you can settle down and get some sleep?"

William shrugged his head from her hand. "I'd sleep now if you'll stop petting me like a pug."

Deborah smiled and gave his head one last tousle. "I'm proud of you, William. You were very brave."

He smiled a sleepy smile as he lay back down on the blankets. "You were brave, too, Aunt Deborah. Really brave."

"Well, let's both keep being brave and pray your da safely home."

He nodded as she rose. She closed the door with a soft

click and headed for the rocking chair, tucking her legs and curling herself tightly into a woolen blanket. The slow back and forth calmed her racing heart, and she felt the exhaustion settle with each creek of the floorboards.

Soon, her eyes were too heavy to be denied. She looked back toward the overcrowded bedroom, then to George's open door.

Did she dare? Sleepiness won out and she wearily made her way to George's bed. She'd die if he found her here when he returned, but it was the best option to get a little rest before morning.

She loosened her stays and lay down on top of his covers, pulling her blanket up under her chin. She was caught off guard by the smell of George on the pillow. Wood and soap, and something that was uniquely him.

She felt the loss of his strong presence so keenly and longed to be able to tell him what was in her heart. What became so clear tonight somewhere in the middle of all the fear and worry. A tear slipped out of her closed eyes, like the tears of women through time who hope hatred won't find those they love.

CHAPTER 29

Deborah awoke with a start with the sun streaming through the window. From the brightness, she knew the morning was well past. She heard sounds coming from the kitchen and felt a blush creep up her neck. Of course, George wouldn't come to bed with her in there. She put herself together and rushed out the door, coming to a halt as she saw Sarah stirring a pot on the stove, Deborah's white apron tied around her waist.

"Oh! Thanks, Sarah. I thought maybe your da was back." Deborah's eyes scanned the room.

"No. William told me all about last night. I can't believe I slept through the whole thing! He went downstairs to clean up the glass." She propped the spurtle on the cast iron pot. "The porridge is almost done, and I lit the fire by myself. I hope that's alright?" Her look was proud and tentative.

Deborah came to the stove and wrapped her in a big hug. "It's more than alright. Aren't you the little lady?" She paused. "There's no sign of your da?"

Sarah shook her head. "No. The house was quiet when I woke up. The rest are sleeping, except William. He said that you were really brave with those two mean men last night, Aunt Deborah."

"I was terrified, luv. But all will be well today." She said the words, but a stone sunk in her stomach. George should be home by now. As if to answer her thought, the door opened. Her heart leaped, but William came through the entrance, his clothes and hair crumpled.

"Aunt Deborah, it's a mess down there. The window is all broke up, and they smashed lots of the furniture. Da's not going to be happy when he comes back home."

"No, he won't. But we're all safe now, and that's what matters," Deborah said.

She turned to Sarah. "Can you get everyone fed, Sarah? William and I will do some clean-up downstairs and then come for our breakfast."

William groaned, but followed Deborah back out the door. The ruin downstairs shocked her, even with William's warning. A bed frame was kicked in half and broken chairs sat in scattered pieces where the mattress should go. Tools littered the floor beside where the workbench was tipped over, and the air had a pungent odor Deborah traced to a can of varnish puddling in the corner.

William tossed a large piece of glass into the garbage bin. "Watch your fingers, William." She picked her way around the rubble and looked out of the hole in the broken window. She fingered a blank painted "C" on the glass, the lone survivor from "Carpenter" that had been stenciled on the window that George had been so proud of. Cold air pricked her face. Down the street, she saw several other devastated storefronts. All Irish. She'd check on the neighbors soon.

With William's help, they nailed scattered pieces of wood across the window opening. The doorknob and lock had been kicked in, but a few nails and additional lumber secured the door. For good measure, they pushed the workbench up against the opening. George would use the back door anyway, and there wouldn't be customers in here for some time. It wouldn't stop anyone bent on getting inside, but she felt more secure. William's stomach growled.

"Let's go feed that belly, William. We'll finish sweeping up the glass later." Deborah said, looking around the hate-torn room.

With the window boarded up, shadows gathered across the demolished furniture and supplies. She fought back tears, thinking of all George's wasted work. She trudged up the stairs behind William.

The morning passed quietly and eventually afternoon shadows threw their light across the floor. They all busied themselves with reading, games, and meal preparation, but the anxiety in the room hovered like a low cloud over everything they did.

As night fell, the street was eerily quiet, the previous evening's fury faded and spent. The sound of a peeler's whistle in the distance occasionally broke the silence, but it seemed Bucklemaker Wynd wore its polite, company-ready face again. "Nothing to see here," it smiled through clenched teeth.

Deborah peeked from behind the lace curtains several times, watching the same lone police officer pace up and down the street, swinging a definitive baton at his side. She didn't recognize the style of his uniform. *Probably peelers brought in from Edinburgh.* The local force had certainly not been adequate to reign in the rage last night. Surely, with law and order restored, George might come back home.

She tried to busy herself with cleaning up dinner but her nerves were taut as the cloth she'd just rung over the basin. "I think I'll go check on Mrs. Carse for a bit," she told the children. They all looked up from their books sluggishly, nodding. "Susannah, it's your turn to play with Debbie. Keep a good eye on her, love." Susannah moved towards her younger sister and picked up one of the small rag dolls Deborah had shaped from leftover scraps of fabric. Their babies were talking to each other as Deborah left.

She stopped by Mary Carse's first. Apart from discomposure towards her countrymen who had caused so much heartache in Dundee, she was well.

Deborah looked down the quiet street, turning away from home. She just couldn't go back yet to where George's absence took up so much space. She walked past littered gutters. Stepped over ripped books. Walked around the broken liquor bottles that had probably inflamed the otherwise staid community.

She climbed the back stairs to talk to Mrs. Coyle, whose husband had been beaten badly. He rested on a makeshift bed by the hearth, eyes swollen shut and sporting three broken ribs.

Deborah hugged the worn woman. "I'm sorry he bore the brunt of last night, Lorna. That must've been quite a scare," she whispered.

"Aye. A scare, but we've not borne the brunt. His brother's pub is all but in shambles. Our dear priest's residence is leveled near to the ground along with the church. And there's talk of three men dead! Lucky, we are. Broken ribs heal in time."

Deborah was still. Or maybe the whole world paused to make room for the news. Somehow, her voice broke the stillness. "Who, Lorna?"

"I don't know, as the authorities aren't giving names out yet. You know, don't want to get everyone all riled up again just when the streets have calmed down. But I heard it from Widow Ballantyne whose son is a peeler. There are three what's not coming home. They've nabbed two men for the murder. A mob like last night and only two in custody! The jails should be full up and more, I say, but at least they caught a couple."

Deborah nodded and muttered something in farewell. She stumbled down the stairs, her hand gripping the railing, searching for something stable to hold on to. The bell startled her as she exited and the cold wind whipped her face.

Is that why George isn't home yet?

The words settled heavily in the air around her. The thought of him lying cold in a morgue constricted her lungs, choking her breath. She took in reluctant air but couldn't stop the tears that squeezed out from her closed eyes.

She ran towards home, her heels clipping the rough cobblestone and echoing down the empty street. A hundred feet away from the shop, she stopped, unable to bring herself to go inside and find he wasn't there. She swallowed hard and put out a hand to steady herself against the brick. She leaned her back against the roughness, welcoming the cold. She closed her eyes and was consumed with images of George. His gentle smile. His hearty laugh. And those eyes, so full of life. Compassion. Mirth. Love. For the children. For her.

Her thoughts continued back to Ireland when he'd told her his first secret on the lane by the orchard, and through the last year, when she'd kept her secrets far too well.

Surely it couldn't be too late to tell him. Now that she finally knew.

"I hope those sweet little tears aren't on my account." She felt work-worn fingers brush a stray tear from her cheek and looked up, eyes wide, at George's smiling face. He looked a little tattered and smudges of dirt littered his handsome face, but he was safe. He was back.

Deborah grabbed the rough cloth of his shirt and pulled him to her, burying her face in the smell of wood and sweat and safety as sobs overtook her frame.

"Shhh. It's all over now, luv." He pulled her close and rested his chin on her head.

"They came...and you didn't come back...and Mrs. Coyle said..." She tried talking, tried telling him everything in her heart, but all the worry from the past day gushed out in her choked tears.

He shushed her again and just held her. "Tell me when you're all done watering my shirt, dearie."

She pulled him even tighter, snaking her arms around his middle, burrowing into his strength. He kissed the top of her head again and stroked her back in lazy circles with gentle comfort.

Soon, her breathing slowed and her pulse returned to normal. She relaxed her grip on his tear-sodden shirt, and lay her head on his chest, listening to his strong and steady heartbeat.

He let out a long breath. "Are you all well? That was the longest night of my life, so full of worry for you."

"We're all just fine. The mob did come looking for you.

They did some damage and rattled everyone, but they left without harming us." Deborah pulled back a few inches to look at him and wiped her face on the back of her sleeve. "But George, when you didn't come back today, I thought you were dead!" Her voice hitched.

He pulled her closer and chuckled, low and quiet. "Ah, that explains it. I knew there had to be some good reason for you to come barreling into my arms." He kissed the top of her head. "I'm sorry you had to go through that alone, but it's good I wasn't home when they came. I've never seen men so out for blood. All around us men were getting lashed, and worse. We wanted to try to help but didn't dare for the size of the mob. We ran for a good two miles out of town, chased the whole way, and spent the night hiding in the brambles like convicts. There were still attacks going on this morning before the extra Edinburgh peelers made it to town and brought order with them."

Deborah exhaled and leaned in again, soaking up his presence.

There was a smile in his voice when he spoke next, low into her ear. "But I'd happily spend the night in the thicket again if it brought me back here, with you hanging on me in broad daylight."

Chagrined, she extracted her hands, smoothing the wet, wrinkled fabric. She sniffed and started to move away, but he pulled her back in.

"As usual, you've handled it all, wonder that you are."

She let out a puff of air. "I'm hardly a wonder. I was so terrified, George. I was scared I'd lost you."

"You *are* a certified wonder, Deb. You dealt single-handedly with a mob, you've handled one crisis after another from personal pain to women in labor, and you've spent the better part of your life taking care of my children in a way that I'm sure has made their mothers bless your name from heaven." He paused for a moment, emotion catching his throat. "Aye. You are a wonder. I'll never be able to repay you for your kindness and sacrifice." He paused, bringing his cheek to hers. His voice was low in her ear. "All I can offer is to love you for the rest of my life. If you'll have me."

The emotion built between them with a slow warmth that seemed to fill every part of her. When he spoke again against her ear, his words were ragged and low. "Deborah, I want you to be my wife."

She pulled back to meet his fiery eyes. "I do want to be your wife, George." She paused. "I think I'm ready," she said in a voice barely above a whisper.

"I know it is rushing things a bit, lass." He leaned in with a smile and lowered his voice. "We've only been married for just over a year."

A little giggle came out more like a choke. She pressed her forehead against his chest.

George chuckled. "For being the most courageous woman this side of the Irish Sea, you sure are easy to scare off." He kissed the top of her head and ran his hand along her back as he pulled her closer again, her head resting on his pounding heart. "Deborah, please tell me I'm not alone in this."

She hesitated, then slowly shook her head against his shirt. "George, I love you, too. Truly."

This time, his laugh was deep and full. "Well! It's about time!"

He bent down and swung her up into his arms. He took her a few steps further into the darkness of the alleyway and deposited her in the alcove of a deserted store.

Mischief filled his smile. "Now, wife of mine, I'm going to kiss you unless you have any further objections." He lowered his head toward her and cocked an eyebrow.

Deborah shook her head.

"You're sure?"

She nodded.

His mouth sought hers softly until she stepped into the last few inches and melted to him. He smiled into the kiss and pulled her even closer.

Her hands traveled from his chest up to his neck to finger the curls there, solving her question about how his hair would feel between her fingers. She stroked his silky locks as he broke away to kiss her forehead, her cheeks, her neck, and then back to her lips, finishing the kiss so gently that she felt tears prick. When he pulled away, she was breathing heavier than after her run through the cobbled streets.

George put his arms against the door frame and took a deep breath. "Will you truly marry me, sweet Deborah?" He touched his head to hers. "And be my wife."

"I did. And I will." A wide grin lit up his face and she raised on her tiptoes and kissed his nose.

He laughed as he pulled her off her feet in an embrace, then took her hand and led her home.

CHAPTER 30

The reunion was a joyful one, with tears and laughter to go around. It was a struggle to calm everyone enough to sleep, but Deborah finally heard the girl's breathing slow into a steady rhythm.

She sat at the small dressing table opposite the window and unbraided her hair. She picked up a hairbrush, stroking her long locks until they crackled, then set the brush down noiselessly. A long beam of moonlight came through her window, enough to look herself over in the small mirror that sat on the bureau. She wore her best nightgown, but it was yellow and faded. *Not much notice to collect my trousseau.*

She could hardly read what was in her own eyes. After becoming a bride over a year ago, was she ready to be a wife? A small smile came without thought, images of the past day filling her mind. The worry. The fear. His surprising kisses.

His surprising love. Her surprising life.

Rising, she opened the door silently and noiselessly padded across the dark room. She stood outside George's door, raised her hand, and lowered it again. *Do I knock? Go right in?* She took a slow breath and put her forehead against the smooth wood. One knock and everything would change. They would change. She breathed again, smelling the pine. Hearing the silence of the house and the sleeping world outside. Feeling the cold wood beneath her bare feet. Listening to her heartbeat, hard and strong against her chest.

"It's much warmer in here, you know." The voice came from right behind the door. She startled, then let out a small giggle, covering her mouth with her hand.

"That's why I'm out here," she teased, then bit her lip.

He chuckled. "I'd bet those funny-looking little toes are pretty chilly. Why don't you come on in and let me warm them up for you?"

She paused, silent. She could barely breathe, let alone think of something witty to say. She put her hand flat on the wood, imagining his pressed on the other side. Could he hear her heart beating from there?

"Knowing you're standing there in just a wee nightgown is killing me, luv. I said I'd never open your door, and I'll keep that promise. But I'd be the happiest Irishman in Scotland if you'd open mine."

She heard his footsteps move away, towards his bed.

Away from her. She put her hand on the knob and pushed the door open.

Deborah stood at the stove, stirring porridge with a wooden spurtle. A slow smile spread across her face as she glanced at the workshop door. She could hear George working below, but hadn't seen him this morning. She woke up in his bed alone to hear the sounds of his planer scraping across wood, disoriented for a moment. She rolled over to his pillow and smelled the faint smell of him that lingered there. She had slipped into the girls' room to fetch her dress before they woke and changed her clothes in George's room. Her room. She felt like a trespasser as she hurriedly slipped her nightgown over her head and opened the top bureau drawer. It was mostly full of his clothes, but she carefully folded the white fabric and placed it on top of his shirts.

All sorts of things to work out. But some things last night worked out just fine.

She could tell she was blushing, just remembering. She heard footsteps behind the door and she put her hand over her heart, willing it to quiet.

What did she say to him? What did married people do?

She drew in her breath as the door opened and she saw George brushing the sawdust off his clothes onto the rug and slipping off his boots. He looked up and saw her at the stove. A big grin lit his face, and he crossed the distance in two strides. He took the spurtle from her hands, set it down, and pulled her off her feet into his embrace. He kissed her soundly on the lips and set her back down, kissing the top of her head. He stood back to look at her, his eyes sparkling.

"I had the most magical dream last night, sweet Deborah." He pulled her close again, and she buried her head in his shoulder. "I heard these little wee footsteps and then my door opened up to a bit of heaven."

"Funny," she whispered. "I had a similar dream. But when I woke up, I was all alone and didn't know if it was real or not."

"It was hard to drag myself to the shop with you warming up my bed so nice and toasty, but McGregors are coming for their table after lunch. I can't just kiss all day, lass. You've got to let a man get some work in some time."

He grinned as she poked him in the ribs. He tickled her back and grabbed her around the waist. They both startled as the girl's bedroom door opened. Sarah and Susannah came out as George and Deborah quickly separated.

"You didn't sleep in our room last night, Aunt Deborah. I woke up and your blankets were still folded. Where were you?" Sarah asked.

The stairwell door opened as she finished her question. The boys came in, William rubbing his eyes. He looked between George and Deborah, interested in the response.

George looked at Deborah and she sent him a sweet smile, batting her eyelashes, saying nothing. *This one is yours, Da.* "Well, we decided that since you girls snore like banshees and the boys smell like highland coos, the only place Aunt Deborah is going to get any sleep is in my room. So, she's sleeping in my room now." He raised his chin and tried to look natural. "With me."

The girls shrugged and started debating who would get Deborah's bed and patchwork blanket now. A slow smile began on William's face as he looked between the adults, standing with deliberate nonchalance. "Well, that seems to be the only option, then. How kind you are, Da."

George looked at him and raised an eyebrow. "Aye. That I am. Now go wash up." He tousled William's hair as he walked by, grinning from ear to ear. James followed, getting a kiss from Deborah on his way to the basin.

She turned. "Come sit up, girls. Sarah, please go and get Debbie. I hear her waking up."

Soon, everyone settled down at the table, a steaming pot of porridge in the middle. George took her hand as they readied for grace. As he prayed, she looked around the morning-mussed group, joy flowing into all the cracked places left inside. This was her beautiful family. This was her beautiful life.

Her eyes rested on George, his head bowed in prayer. She couldn't hold back the smile that took over her face. He paused and opened his eyes, sensing her gaze. He grinned and winked at her, then continued on with his prayer.

Grace, indeed.

EPILOGUE

ONE YEAR LATER

The sun streamed through the window, diffused by the white curtain that rippled softly in the breeze. Deborah reached for the cradle next to the bed, where her baby just spent her first night. George stirred beside her as she lifted the tiny bundle of jet-black hair and white blankets to nestle under her chin.

George rolled over and smiled, fingering a tuft of the baby's soft hair. Deborah sighed. "I should let her sleep, but she looks so beautiful in the sunlight."

He rose in bed and kissed Deborah on her forehead. "She is beautiful indeed, and so are you. How are you feeling this morning, little Momma, after your spectacular performance yesterday?"

Deborah smiled. "Sore. Tired. Content. Glad it's over.

Glad she's here." She looked over at George and rested her head against his shoulder. "Glad you're here."

"I'm glad, too." He kissed the top of her head. "So, what will you be calling this pretty wee package?"

Deborah took a breath and looked away. She started slowly. "I'm not sure how you'll feel about this, and it's fine if it's not fine, but it would mean a lot to me. I would like...," she paused, looking him in the eye to make sure she read his first reaction. "I want to name her Rebecca."

George sighed, his eyes glistening immediately as he touched his head to hers. "Oh, Deborah. Only you." He took the baby's tiny hand that had fussed its way out of the blankets and rubbed its tiny whiteness with his brown, calloused finger. "What do you think, sweet babe? Would you like to be called after your lovely auntie who planned all this happiness for us?"

The baby tucked her legs to her belly, bringing her other fist to her mouth and sucking noisily. They both chuckled softly and George drew Deborah in to meet his warm kiss. He pulled back with a sigh and looked again at the squirming bundle.

"Well, wee one, it looks like you'll have Rebecca's name and your mother's appetite."

Deborah elbowed him but smiled, even as the tears flowed down her face. Healing. Cleansing. "Thank you, George. For the name. Deborah and Rebecca will be sisters again." She kissed the downy head tucked under her chin.

"How did she know?" George asked softly. "How did she know we needed each other?"

Deborah fingered the gold ring on her left hand, letting the joy and sadness settle a little before she spoke. "Rebecca was always one step closer to heaven than either of us. I admit I was dismayed when she asked me to be your wife, but when we married that day, I felt a little of that heaven, too. I felt a goodness and peace that reminded me of her. I still don't know how so much happiness can find its way out of the shadows of pain, but I'm so glad it can." She turned and gently pressed her lips to his. "I'm so glad it did."

George swallowed and nodded. He pulled Deborah and the baby close, wrapping them in his arms as sunlight from the window flooded them with warmth.

THE END

AUTHOR'S NOTES

I've loved taking this journey with my courageous great-great-great grandmother, Deborah Ann Hasley Wright. Her sister Rebecca died on September 2, 1843. According to family documents, she called Deborah to her bedside and made her promise to marry George and care for her family after she died. She gave Deborah her ring and earrings and asked her to honor her last wish. I imagined what events would cause Deborah to be willing to marry her brother-in-law, mere weeks after her sister's death. I wondered what it would have been like to become the stepmother to Rebecca's and Ellen's children. And I especially wondered if she ever fell in love with her husband. Those questions eventually led me to research this remarkable story.

As I read historical newspapers to learn about the world of Dundee Scotland at the time Deborah lived there, I was swept up in the religious and racial tensions that boiled over into riots, and the epidemics that shook their community. Or, maybe that's what I noticed in the papers because that's what was swirling around my family and me in 2020. This book took on a life of its own, as I saw so many of the same problems in 19th-century Scotland on my own evening news. I was blown away by the derogatory remarks printed about the Irish, in books and newspapers of the time. In my simplistic historical education, I always thought that the

Potato Famine (1845-1849) and subsequent migration caused much of the anti-Irish sentiment throughout Europe and America. But it was the other way around. For years, the public had been told that the Irish were lazy, indolent, and inferior. When the famine hit, people were primed to blame the victims for their predicament. So, they looked the other way as millions perished. I can't count the times during the writing of this book that I read a racially-charged Facebook post, heard a politician or newscaster make a subtle derogatory remark about another group of people, or saw victim-blaming behind public policy decisions about immigration. Truly, 'Man's inhumanity to man makes countless thousands mourn.'

Even with reliving so many historical parallels, writing a romance was a great stress reliever for me in the middle of homeschooling, working remotely, and dealing with the stress we all experienced during the COVID-19 pandemic. It was a bright spot to walk this journey with Deborah and imagine what her path looked like. Thanks for strolling along with me.

I always appreciate help sorting out the fact/fiction salad. Deborah Ann Hasley (or Hazley) was born on May 14, 1818, in Newry, County Down, Ireland. Her sister Rebecca was born ten years earlier, in 1808. George was born in 1807. There is much written about her by her children, and many details in the book are straight from their personal histories and historical documents. Rebecca and Deborah appear to have lost their mother in 1822 when Deborah was 4 and Rebecca was 14. Their father lived until 1866 and died in Ireland, according to Ireland's Civil Registration, but some of the details are hazy.

Family histories can be funny things. They provide so many important details, but sometimes miss the facts because they are written years after an event, because memories change and fade, or even because events were modified on purpose. For example, Deborah was described by Ellen and Rebecca's children as "the best of stepmothers" and a woman who tried to give her children the best education possible. Great details! But in many histories of the Wright family, including one written in adulthood by William, it is reported that Deborah helped with the Wright children and then honored her sister's wish by marrying George one year later. Historical documents don't support this. The marriage license from Dundee shows George and Deborah marrying on November 20, 1843, just weeks after Rebecca's death on September 2 of the same year. I wondered if there was a time when they married in name only to care for the children, then found romantic love later. To a child's mind, realizing that their parents were now living together as man and wife could form a memory that they married a year later. Or, maybe a child wouldn't want to say "on the record" that his father remarried so soon after his mother died. I'll never know.

The George Wright family moved several times. I've

centered the story in just two locations, County Down Ireland, and Dundee Scotland. In 1841, The Wrights lived at 20 Bucklemaker Wynd in Dundee, where George was listed on census records as a furniture broker, carpenter, or joiner. In fact, the last name "Wright" indicates a worker or shaper of wood. George's shop shared a location with the family residence. Deborah was trained as a midwife and practiced in Dundee. Dundee was also the place of Rebecca's death and burial at Howff Cemetery and George and Deborah's wedding. The children included in the story are George's real children, but (alas!) I didn't have the skill or space to include all of them. Rebecca did have a daughter right before she passed away, and named her Deborah, after her sister. Two years after Rebecca's death, George and Deborah named their first child, a daughter, Rebecca. The fact that they named their daughters after each other just melts my heart and cements in my mind the love these sisters must have had for each other.

Charlie is a name I got from a ship register of the time, but this character is fictional. (Though I'm sure some of you recognize him...Handsome. Charming. Bad news.) Many of the other characters in the book are from historical sources including the Dundee Post Office Directory of 1843. Mary Carse was a widow on Bucklemaker Wynd on a pension, Caroline Bethune was a Scottish midwife (or howdie), Walter Moyle had a hatting establishment, and James Chalmer did in fact own a bookstore. He took out an ad in the 1843 Dundee Post Office Directory advertising items such as penknives, drawing colours, fifes, flute music, globes, and journals. It sounds like somewhere I'd have liked to visit! I don't know his views on the Irish, but I do know that he later invented the adhesive postage stamp (in case you're ever on Jeopardy).

The Castle Theatre was a prominent cultural establishment in Dundee. Ira Aldridge is a fascinating historical figure. He did perform in Dundee and across Europe to much acclaim. He was known for his role as Othello. When putting on make-up for another role he once said, "It is easy to make a white man black, but it is a dirty job to make a black man white."

The *Dundee Courier* was a weekly newspaper and can be accessed online. During this period, there were several extraordinarily negative articles published about the Irish. One of the quotes in the book is from the *Dundee Courier* on Tuesday 16 January 1844.

Another great resource was a delightful book called *Dundee Worthies* by George Martin. The book contains interviews with Dundee's old-timers in the late 1800s and early 1900s who reflect on the interesting people and places of their childhood in Dundee. It is a true gift from past to present. It paints a vivid picture of Jamie May standing for hours on Perth Road, watching the "prettily dressed maidens and their beaux pass by" on Sunday afternoons or children chanting the rhyme for Jenny Marshall's Candy:

"When going along the Nethergate / There's naught can be so handy, O, / As dropping in to get a stick / Of Jenny Marshall's candy, O." I was excited, after writing the fortune-teller scene, to find an account of a real fortune-teller who lived during this time in Dundee named Spunk Janet. She catered to "old maids, wanton widows, and impatient lasses." Likewise, many other details about Dundee, such as the attractions at the Greenmarket, are all real, as is the Physick Paddy O'Neil. He and others like him were practicing "cures" that included some pretty crazy prescriptions. If you'd like a wart removed with a bit of historical quackery, just carry a joint of straw in your hand and find out where a funeral is taking place. At the first movement of the hearse, then pulled by horses, throw the straw underneath the procession and your warts will fade. (You're welcome!)

Medical books of the time suggest that a new illness ravaged Dundee in 1842-1844 that was originally thought to be influenza. A similar epidemic came through Edinburgh in 1843, with a mortality rate of 1 in 20. The treatments in the book were prescribed to patients. I was impressed with the research done during this period and gathered information on the epidemiology of the time from *The Edinburgh Medical and Surgical Journal* (1845), *The Edinburgh Medical Journal* (1859), and *The British and Foreign Medical Review* (1844). Rebecca's cause of death is listed as influenza. That could have been the cause, but there were other epidemics in the area at the time that were frequently put under that umbrella because they didn't have names for the new diseases. Rebecca is buried at the Howff Cemetery in Dundee.

From *Undiscovered Dundee* by Brian King, I learned about the infamous race riots in Dundee. The boxing match, pub fight, and resulting race riot took place as described in Dundee, but it occurred in 1830. The tensions between the Irish and Scottish lasted for decades but never reached this level of devastation again. The same book also gave me the background for Deborah and George's trip to Invergowrie. The large boulders there are the subject of a famous prophecy by Thomas the Rhymer in the thirteenth century. 'When the Goors of Gowrie come to land / The Day of Judgement's near at hand.' So far, so good.

This has been a tasty journey. The recipes in the book are some of my favorites. If you want to dine like it's 1826, head over to Margaret Dods's *The Cook and Housewife's Manual Containing the Most Approved Modern Receipts* on Google Books. It is always a trip to find substitutes for some of the ingredients. If you are out of "good shin beef," and "large old fowls" for your cock-a-leekie soup, you'll do fine with stock and chicken breast.

Another great book available online is by Alice Bertha from 1894. Just the title itself makes me smile: *The traditional games of England, Scotland and Ireland: with tunes, singing rhymes and methods of playing according* to the variants extant and recorded in different parts of the kingdom. Here I found the game Johnny Rover (give it a go!) and one of the first recorded instances of the song *I'll Tell Me Ma* or *The Belle of Belfast City*. Newry is about 38 miles from Belfast, so it's possible George knew the song.

I consider the beautiful poetry of Robert Burns a cameo character in this book. Rebecca, the first daughter of Deborah and George, wrote that she grew up with a love for the songs and poems of Robert Burns. I was happy to attribute that love to her mother Deborah and include it in this book. All Burns poems are kept in the original "Scots" form, with slight modifications when the meaning would be unclear. The following poems are used in the story: "To a Mouse," "A Fiddler in the North," "Bess and her Spinning Wheel," "Auld Lang Syne," "Man was made to Mourn," and "A Red, Red Rose." I found a beautiful, water-damaged book of Burns poetry from 1839 on eBay. I like to look at the tattered brown tome and imagine a passionate soul like Deborah picking it up in a bookstore on the streets of Dundee, holding it to her heart, and bringing it home to read by firelight. As I do the same, I think of her.

TIME OR TIDE BOOKCLUB

Music

Create a fun atmosphere by playing music from Scotland. Try searching Burns: The Complete Collection (produced by Linn Records) on your streaming service or scan below to order on Amazon. These are some of the best recordings of Burn's words. Right now, I'm listening to "Lassie wi' the Lintwhite Locks" from Volume 3. I'd love to share it!
Point your phone's camera at the QR code below to order.

Favors

Consider providing favors that go along with the book. Print quotes from Robbie Burns poetry or purchase a paperback copy of his poetry for each member. Scan QR for a pocket copy of Burns.

Food

Serve book-inspired snacks! If you'd like, print a recipe card for everyone in your book club. Download printable cards at www.alisonbensonmoulton.com.

PETTICOAT TAILS

These slightly-sweet treats are simple and delicious. They get their name from the shape of hoop petticoats. The ingredients and instructions are from an 1826 cookbook.

Ingredients

10 Tbsp real butter, melted
1 1/2 c. all-purpose flour
1/2 c. sugar
Pinch of salt

Directions

- Mix this, "but not too much"
- Press or roll out to the shape of a dinner plate on a baking sheet or pizza stone.
- "Cut a cake from the centre of this, with a large tumbler. Keep the inner circle whole, and cut the other one into eight petticoat-tails."
- Crimp edges like a pie crust, or press with a fork. Prick surface with a fork.
- Bake at 350 degrees for 12-15 minutes, removing before it browns.
- "Serve the round cake in the middle of the plate, and petticoat-tails round it."
- The traditional add-in is caraway seeds, but 1/2 tsp. vanilla, lemon, or almond extract are more pleasing to modern tastes. We won't tell if you add nuts or chocolate chips, either!

CRANACHAN

Derived from a Scottish breakfast food called crowdie, cranachan is a light and simple treat perfect for any time of day.

Ingredients

2 c. fresh or frozen raspberries
½ c. oats
5 Tbsp honey, divided
1 1/2 c. heavy whipping cream

Directions

- Spread oats in a layer on a baking sheet. Bake at 350 F for 10 minutes until very light brown.
- In a small bowl, toss the raspberries with 1 Tbsp honey, crushing a few raspberries into a puree.
- Whisk the cream on medium-high speed on a hand or stand mixer until just starting to thicken. Turn off the mixer and add 4 Tbsp honey. Whip until soft peaks form.
- In a glass bowl, trifle dish, or individual serving dishes, layer the ingredients as desired or gently combine.
- If desired, top with a sprinkle of oats, and a few whole raspberries.

DISCUSSION QUESTIONS

1. How did the setting influence this story?

2. How did poetry and music feature in the plot? Was there a poem that resonated with you?

3. Could you relate to the cultural conflicts? What similarities did you see between events you've experienced and the ones described in the book?

4. *Time or Tide* discusses losing a family member. If you've experienced this tragedy, how did you relate to the emotions and actions of the characters? How was their experience like or unlike yours?

5. If you could have lunch with any character in this book, who would you invite and why?

6. This book features a non-traditional romance between George and Deborah. Did you anticipate it? How did you feel about their growing love?

7. What do you think of the phrase "Only Luve"? Do you think people have one true soulmate?

8. Deborah is passionate. Do you think it is a weakness or strength in this story?

9. What would you have done in Deborah's position? Do you think she made the best choice? What other options could she have considered?

11. What character do you relate to the most?

12. Have you known someone like Charlie? What "red flags" stood out to you about his character?

13. Why do you think Deborah liked Charlie? Why do you think she fell in love with George?

14. How do you balance the practical and the emotional when making a difficult decision?

15. There are many transitions in this book. Ambiguous transition points where the threshold lines are blurred are sometimes called "liminal." The story has many liminal moments, such as transitions between life and death, water and shore, friendship and romantic love, or day and night. Did any of these moments of change stand out to you? Did you relate to any of them?

16. Are there any lines you marked in the book?

17. How would you adapt this book into a movie? Who would you cast in the starring roles?

18. Do you read the author notes at the end of historical fiction? Do the author's notes in *Time or Tide* enhance this story for you?

19. If there was a prequel or sequel to this book, what storyline or people would you want to know more about?

20. If you were to write a story about one of your ancestors, what would the plot be?

Love and thanks to...

Cecelia and Vaughn
for encouraging me to share my words

Paul
for better-than-fiction kisses

McKay, Zachary, Emma, Lizzy, Brigham
for giving me so many reasons to smile

Sabrina and Sophia
for expanding my family and my heart

Beta readers and online writing groups
for collective wisdom and support

And to you, my dear readers, thanks for picking up Deborah's story and spending time with me. There are millions of books to choose from; I'm so grateful you choose this one.

ABOUT THE AUTHOR

Ali loves words. Her favorite word is *lollygag*. Her least favorite word is *laundry*. She likes to wrangle stray words into stories, songs, poems, and plays. Ali leads Baby Storytime at her local library, reading board books and rocking out with the teething crowd with the only four chords she knows on the ukulele. She's published a children's book (*When Mommy's Home with Me*), several plays, and songs that range from country ballads to preschool clean-up songs. Ali graduated from Brigham Young University in Human Development and English.

At any given time, she can be found perusing Victorian phone books for names, scouring vintage cookbooks for recipes, and sighing over 19th-century fashion plates. Her favorite place in the world is at home with her growing family, their naughty goats, too many rescue cats, and a Great Pyrenees who will do anything for haggis.

Come connect!

instagram.com/vintageauthorali

facebook.com/moultonalison

alisonbensonmoulton.com

Made in the USA
Columbia, SC
10 October 2023